CW00430253

ESCAPE FROM ESTONIA

RICHARD WAKE

MANOR AND STATE, LLC

PART I

1

The island's name was Suomenlinna. It was in the harbor outside Helsinki, an old fortress that had mostly turned into a place for tourists and picnics and kids running around on the weekend. It was actually several islands in a group but, well, whatever. At least, that was what old Antti told me. Myself, I had never seen it in daylight, never seen it as anything but dark and desolate.

I thought of Antti as the Ancient Mariner, except he seemed older. His face was brown and wrinkled from the sun, like an old leather glove that had dried after being left out in the rain. His boat seemed nearly as old as the man, but the engine always ran quietly and there was never a hint of a leak. Those were the main requirements, seeing as how Antti's job was to ferry me across the Gulf of Finland in secret, from Tallinn to Suomenlinna and then back again.

It was about two hours each way, give or take, depending upon the weather. Fifty miles — at least, that was about what it looked like on a map. This night, it was early November and already frigid on the water.

"A little early for the snot to be frozen to my face, old man," I said.

"You could just blow your nose."

"Forgot a handkerchief."

"Sleeves work in a pinch."

"Don't think so. This is a new coat."

"Then stop bitching about a little frozen snot," Antti said. "This is nothing. In January, there are going to be goddamned icicles hanging from our nostrils. Real stalagmites."

"Stalactites — they're the ones that hang from the roof," I said.

"Same difference," Antti said. "Snot is snot."

Then he muttered, "Knowitallasshole," all mushed together in one word. Despite that, I thought he liked me. I knew he liked the wad of cash I brought him every two weeks. It was more than he made from fishing, a lot more — of that, I was certain.

The wind was against us, which would add close to a half-hour to the trip. We would fly home, though, and that was the way I preferred it. The upside of being against the wind was that, when I ducked down into the little open cabin below the steering wheel, I was sheltered from the worst of the weather. But it was still freezing, and despite the long underwear — also new, and more than a bit itchy — I could barely stop shivering.

Antti wasn't much of a talker, which was fine with me — more time to bitch to myself about what exactly I was doing on the boat in the first place. My controller was named Gerhard, and he was in Helsinki, and he said I had to bring my information to him — that was the short version. The truth was, it was the only version that mattered. The rest of it wasn't worth saying out loud, but it was fine to have it ping-ponging around in my brain, bouncing around, only to have the thought interrupted by Antti's one-word pronouncement: "Incoming."

I had learned on earlier voyages that this was the old man's announcement that he was about to release the kind of from-the-depths fart that only old men seemed capable of producing. That was my cue to get out of the little dugout directly beneath the steering wheel and return to the fresh, snot-freezing air. Given the wind, I figured they would smell it in Estonia within the hour.

"All clear," Antti announced when his store of ammunition had been depleted. His face bore the look of a craftsman after a job well done.

"You going to tell me this time?" he said.

"Why do you even want to know?"

"Just natural curiosity."

"Could be dangerous to know."

"More dangerous than ferrying a spy across the gulf?" he said. "I don't think so. If they catch me, they're not going to bother with questions, other than the pickup point in Tallinn and the delivery point on the island. One question, two questions, and then two bullets in the head."

"I don't know," I said.

"Humor an old man."

So, I told him. And his reaction was the same as my reaction when I first received the assignment. His reaction was the same three words that had been bouncing around in my brain.

"Fucking train schedules?" Antti said.

"Fucking train schedules," I said.

"And that's worth the money and the danger and..."

"Tell me about it," I said.

"Hey, look."

Antti was pointing in the direction of some kind of wall with an opening in it. You could see it because the moon was shining just right.

"See that? They call it the King's Gate. Nice spot of deep water. Nice stable dock."

"So, why can't we go there?"

"Because they patrol there, idiot," he said.

"But we're on the same side as them."

"We've been through this — you don't want to have to explain yourself to anyone, friend or foe, am I right?"

"Right, right," I said.

"I know I don't want to have to explain myself to anyone," Antti said, more to himself than to me. Then, after a few seconds, a muttered, "Idiot."

We were still more than a mile offshore. After a few minutes, we passed an old gun emplacement that you could see in silhouette against the night sky.

"Been there since the Crimean War," Antti said.

"Which side did you fight on in that one?"

"You know, I'm not that much older than you are."

"Somebody should tell that to your face."

"The face of an honest man doing honest work."

"The face of a smuggler — and if it isn't me, it's some other stolen stuff."

"Just a humble fisherman," he said. "I am offended you would think otherwise."

Pause.

"Incoming."

Two weeks ago, my task was counting ships in the port of Tallinn. Two weeks before that, it was trucks in and out of the prison. This time, it was train schedules — when they arrived, and when they left, and what direction they were heading between the hours of 2 a.m. and 6 a.m. Which meant that I sat on a hill with a vantage point of the rail yard and looked through a tiny telescope and counted train cars in the middle of the night. If I could read any numbers on the side of the locomotives, all the better.

On the one hand, I understood that there could be value in the information. The Gehlen Organization was valuable to the

Americans because we had operatives in places they didn't, places like Tallinn. The more information we could supply the Americans, the greater our value to them and, theoretically, the greater the funding they would send to us. And, well, train schedules suggested troop movements, and material supplies, and whatever else it took the Soviets to keep control of a satellite state like Estonia. I guessed that was worth knowing.

"But why not a radio?" I asked Gerhard. "It's the middle of the 20th century, after all."

"Too dangerous," he said.

"We have really small radios now — you'd be surprised."

"Too dangerous."

"Like a boat in the middle of the night is safe?"

"No radios," Gerhard said.

"Well, I guess you're the boss."

"Fucking right, I'm the boss" he said. "And there's no guessing about it."

About 20 minutes after we saw the King's Gate, Antti began to move closer to the island. The same as the other times, we approached a quiet little cove that, like most of the rest of the coastline, was full of big rocks that could tear a boat like Antti's in half. That was why, about 200 feet out, he dropped a rubber dingy into the water and tossed a rope ladder over the side. That's how I would go the final distance. The first time, I capsized the thing. The next two, I took on enough water that my feet and pants were soaked for the trip back to Tallinn.

I looked over the side and said, "I say we chance the King's Gate."

"I say you learn how to maneuver the dingy better. I mean, really. You're a grown man and you're embarrassing yourself."

Within two minutes, there was a foot of water in the dingy. I was soaked from the waist down by the time I maneuvered it onto the beach.

2
_____

My controller's full name was Gerhard Grimm, and he was sitting on the same rock about a hundred feet onshore as he had been the previous times. My notes on the train schedules and whatnot were written in pencil on some heavy paper, and the sheets were rolled in an oilcloth to protect them in case I ended up in the drink. He unrolled them from the cloth and gave it back to me, and then he stuffed the papers in his breast pocket.

"Anything else?" he said.

"Lot of trains."

"Anything besides trains?"

"Trains are what you asked for. Trains are what I gave you. Times of arrival of trains. Times of departure of trains. Numbers of cars in the trains. Numbers stenciled on the locomotives of the trains. Trains out the ass. Trains, like you asked for."

"No other observations? No personal initiative taken? Nothing like that?"

"You asked for trains," I said.

Gerhard did not reply, other than with a look of disdain that appeared even more negative in the shadows of the night.

"So, what's next?" I said. "Goulash recipes from the officers' wives? Toilet habits of the general staff? Your wish is my command."

"You're damn right, it is."

"Heil Grimm," I said, and gave him the Nazi salute. He had been a colonel in the Wehrmacht, and he just smelled like a Nazi. The man who recruited me into the Gehlen Organization, Fritz Ritter, insisted that there were no high-level Nazis in what was a German-based intelligence outfit.

"So, no swastika tattoos on any of their asses, right?" I said.

"You know it's complicated," Ritter said. "You know, I was in the party."

"But you worked to undermine them — I know that, too," I said. "But the rest of these krauts, I mean..."

"Gehlen isn't a Nazi, I swear," Ritter said. "Nobody with any power is a Nazi. But if one or two at the lower levels had some sympathies..."

"Have some sympathies," I said.

"Maybe have," Ritter said. "Maybe a little. Maybe at the lowest levels. But we need the bodies in certain places. It's a balancing act. Some of these, they're nasty places. And we need some people..."

"Who are nasty," I said.

"Exactly."

"And if they're nasty Nazis, oh well?"

Ritter and I had had this conversation a dozen times in a dozen different ways, both while he was recruiting me and after. And If I understood his perspective, I thought it important to make sure he never forgot the contradictions in his position. Because, while I believed him about Gehlen not being a Nazi, the rest of it was beyond murky. And I had seen too many Nazis up close, both working in Czech intelligence before the war and then for the French Resistance during the war, to permit the murkiness to exist without comment.

"A balancing act," Fritz Ritter said. "And, on balance, I really do believe we are the good guys."

And, on balance, I really did believe that Gerhard Grimm was one of the lower-level agents who still had some Nazi sympathies. I mean, I couldn't prove it, and I was basing it mostly on the fact that he treated me like shit, but there it was.

The thing was, I had never had a controller before other than Ritter. In the past, he had given me my instructions and I was pretty much a free agent, maneuvering as I pleased in pursuit of the overall mission. This one was so different that I almost refused the assignment. Ritter essentially shamed me into going to Tallinn.

"What, you're too good for Estonia?"

"It's not that," I said.

"I can't run every operation directly. I especially can't run the ones that are so far away, and so close to the Soviet border. It's a fact that this business gets trickier the closer you get to Mother Russia — it just does. Estonia is a complicated place, too, and, I mean, it's just best overseen by someone with specialist knowledge. In this case, that's not me. We have an organization and we have associates that I trust. Gerhard Grimm is someone I trust."

"So, why me?"

"Because you're good on the ground. Because you're good with languages. And, I mean, it's just such an odd place — the Soviets took it, then the Nazis took it, then the Soviets took it back. People were loyal to one side, then the other, then back again. Other people subverted one side, then the other, then back again. Kiss Soviet ass, kiss Nazi ass, kiss Soviet ass again — it's a goddamned circus. You operate well in that kind of situation."

"Enough with the ass-kissing."

"It's all true," Ritter said. "And it's not going to be forever. Maybe six months, something like that."

If I wasn't counting the days since I arrived in Tallinn, I still had the calendar in my head. Three more months, give or take. Three more months.

"So, what's next, Herr Obergruppenführer?" I said.

"Go fuck yourself."

"Okay, then. I'll be off."

I stood up, and Grimm said, "Shut up and sit the hell down."

I complied, and he went on to give me my next assignment. He wanted me to get my hands on a roster of employees from the headquarters of something called the MVD.

"Which is?" I said.

"Which is what?"

"The MVD. What the hell is that?"

"It's the Soviet secret police, you idiot."

"That's the NKVD."

"They changed the name."

"Not as far as the Estonians are concerned," I said. "I mean, you'd think that they would have the common courtesy to notify the people they're torturing for information that they've changed their name. I mean, honestly — it's just basic manners. They should tell people — you know, like with a change of address card or something. Because everybody in Tallinn still calls them the NKVD. Usually, to be completely accurate, they call them the fucking NKVD."

"Well, they changed the name."

"And what does it stand for, MVD?"

"The same as NKVD — dank cells and lopped-off pinkies. Christ."

"And you want me to break into Patarei and steal the employment records of everybody who works there?"

"What's Patarei?" Grimm said.

"The NKVD prison."

"Not the prison — the headquarters. The MVD headquarters."

"I have no idea where that is."

Grimm told me the address. It was right in the middle of the
older part of Tallinn. I was pretty sure I had walked by the
building without knowing what it was.

"They're increasing their numbers in the city," Grimm said.
"We're pretty sure about that. What we need is better figures.
What we also need are names. Duty schedules would help, too."

"Is that all?"

"What's the problem, baby?"

"Go fuck yourself," I said. "You've given me no information
about how to get into the secret police headquarters — NKVD,
MVD, whatever the hell. You've given me no idea what I might
find when I get inside. You don't even know if these records
exist."

"They exist," Grimm said. "If they're a military bureaucracy,
they exist. Have you ever known an army that didn't produce
enough paperwork to outweigh the ordinance in the arsenal?"

"They're the secret police, not the army."

"Same difference."

He was likely correct, not that I was going to admit it to him.
Even if they weren't as anal as the Germans — nobody was as
anal about paperwork as the Germans — the Soviets likely had
file cabinets stacked upon file cabinets full of the stuff Grimm
was seeking. But the idea that I was just going to waltz into the
headquarters building and have my run of the file room was
absurd.

"It's not like the Kremlin," Grimm said, dismissing my objec-
tions. "Estonia is an outpost. It's a small damn country. You won't
be breaking into one of the goddamn onion domes on Red
Square. It's just a nothing building in a nothing city in a nothing

country. It's not like the Russkies are sending the cream of the crop to work in Tallinn. It's not like somebody with ambition gets his orders, and sees that they're for Tallinn, and jumps up and down for joy. It's a backwater, which means it's run by back-water-level people. Hell, you might not have to break in. They might invite you in."

"A nothing city in a nothing country, and that's what you've given me for advanced intelligence — nothing. No blueprints. No guard schedules. No location of the files. No nothing."

Grimm didn't answer me. He just stood up from the rock on which he was sitting and dusted off the seat of his pants.

"You're supposed to be good at this — that's what Ritter told me," he said. "So start showing me that you're good at it. Stop being a damn baby. Just get it done."

Grimm walked into the night, in the opposite direction from where I would head, to the side of the island that faced Helsinki. Presumably, that was where he would be picked up — or, maybe he piloted his own boat. Whatever. I stood up and walked back toward where I had beached the dingy. As I walked, the wind was cold on my still-soaked trousers.

3

My typical work day at the warehouse began at about 11 a.m. I discovered quickly that when your job involved the distilling and distribution of bootleg vodka, 11 a.m. qualified as an early hour. That the workers sampled the product went without saying, which was what mostly led to the later starting time. Drink up, stay up, roll in at 11 a.m. — those were the perquisites you received when you toiled full-time in an entirely illegal enterprise.

The rest of the crew drank together a couple of nights a week, and I tried to join them and fit in as best as I could. My Estonian was north of rudimentary but far from fluent. Their German, given the Nazi presence during the war, tended to be about the same. One of the bosses, Artur, spoke in English, and he and I tended to go that way when we were talking. It was fun for both of us to practice our English, and it pissed off the rest of them when we did it, and that made it doubly enjoyable.

I hadn't been able to go out the previous night, though, what with my latest journey to Suomenlinna. Artur was already in the office when I arrived, and he filled me in on what I had missed.

"Olev's girlfriend is pregnant," Artur said. "He's unhappy

about that, and his wife is really unhappy about that. I think he's sleeping on Maksim's sofa for the foreseeable future. That was the big news. The rest was just the normal shit."

"Full attendance?"

"No Linna."

I arched an eyebrow in the time-honored dirty fashion.

"Beats me," Artur said. "If she's smiling when she comes in, maybe."

"And you? Maybe you met her after? Her and that spectacular ass of hers? Here, let me sniff your fingers."

"Not me, brother," Artur said. "She's in a different league. I just drink with the other assholes."

Linna arrived a few minutes later. She was not smiling. In fact, the door was barely closed behind her when she began barking at Ruubert, whose job it was to organize the return of used vodka bottles in exchange for a deposit. I couldn't hear what her complaint was, but I did hear the end, when Linna yelled, "It's always the same shit with you! Always the same shit!"

At which point, Artur and I looked at each other across the warehouse floor. He theatrically covered his crotch with both hands, and I burst out laughing. At the same time, Linna breezed by and said, "And what are you laughing at? Don't you have a delivery route schedule to be finishing so we can get rid of this shit?"

I was one of the delivery guys — there were eight of us on four trucks and a smaller van. On the other side of the wall that divided the warehouse, six men did the distilling and the bottling. There was a full-time mechanic to keep the machinery and the trucks in working order. Ruubert had a half-dozen kids working on the bottle return business, and a half-dozen more who washed out the empties. Artur counted the money, kept the books, and was in charge when Linna wasn't around. Only he could never quite pull off the necessary snarl to keep the menagerie in some kind of order, and it did take a snarl. It was an illegal business, after all. It wasn't as if it attracted choir boys when a job came open — and after a person was hired, he tended to be hungover at least half of the time, which amplified his natural recalcitrance.

"Is the van loaded?" Linna yelled in my direction.

"Not sure."

"Well, would you fucking look?"

I walked across the warehouse floor. There was, indeed, a shipment in the back of the van.

"Looks like eight cases," I said.

"Let's go, you're driving," she said.

"Where to?"

"Across the parking lot."

Across the parking lot was Patarei Prison. Yes, the bootleg vodka operation — maybe the biggest in the city, which meant maybe the biggest in the country — had a parking lot that was contiguous with a massive parking lot and staging area outside of the NKVD prison, or whatever they called themselves.

It seemed absurd, the first time I went to work. It was the first thing I brought up during my job interview with Linna.

"Safest place in the world," she said.

"Huh? How?"

"You can't run an illegal operation of this size without, how do you say, greasing a few palms. You pay off people, important people, for protection. Well, you tell me, who in the entire city of Tallinn can provide better protection than the NKVD? Who, in the entire country of Estonia, can make somebody shit their pants with nothing more than a sideways glance? You have them as a friend, you have the best friend in the world."

"But the cost..."

"Eight cases a week, 35 cases month," Linna said.

"So, 420 cases a year. And 4,200 in a decade. And 30,000 in a nice, long lifetime, give or take."

She waved her hand dismissively.

"Thirty-five cases a month," she said. Another wave. "Like piss down my leg."

"No money? Just vodka?"

"They're Russians, and they're away from home — what can I say? They don't need our money. Vodka and women are what make the Soviet army function."

"Any army," I said.

"Exactly."

The drive might have taken 30 seconds, and that was because I was being careful. We left through the gate of our parking lot, crossed a tiny street, and were waved through the gate of the prison lot. They did not ask for identification. They did not ask us to state our business. There was the slightest hesitation as we approached, but it was only about a half-second before the man in the sentry box waved, ran out, and opened the chain-link gate. The white van from the lot next door was clearly a well-known entity and one that bore gifts.

Linna rolled down her window and yelled at a soldier holding a rifle across his chest, "Baby, go tell your captain that Linna is here." The kid looked embarrassed, and he hesitated for a second, but then the door opened and an older soldier came out. He saw the van and shouted, "Don't keep the lady waiting, asshole." With that, the young soldier sprinted through the door. Within a minute, he returned with his superior officer, presumably the captain.

"Yuri, darling," Linna said. She kissed him on both cheeks, and then she told me, "Open the back so that the captain's men can unload."

I did as I was instructed, and three men — each pushing a hand truck — appeared from behind the door. The choreography suggested pretty strongly that this operation had been performed before.

It didn't take a minute for the three of them to unload the vodka — three cases for the first man, three cases for the second, two cases for the third.

"My office," the captain shouted, interrupting the quiet conversation he was having with Linna with a shout at the hand trucks. I wondered how he doled out the vodka to his men. Was it as a regular ration or as a reward for performance? Or both? I was sure he kept a couple for himself, but that would leave about 90 per week for who-knew-how-many men. It seemed like plenty.

I got back into the van. Two more kisses on the cheek and we were done. I could only wonder if Linna and the captain had another arrangement, besides the vodka — not that I would ever ask.

She jumped in and slammed the door.

"Like piss down my leg," she said. We were back in the warehouse within a minute. She leaned into Artur's office and told him not to forget to book the weekly NKVD payoff that we had just delivered.

"Do you have two sets of books?" I said, after she left.

"No, just the one."

"And you list those eight cases? As what? Under P for Payoffs?"

Artur laughed.

"The vodka goes under 'Spillage,'" he said. "And the bottles go under 'Breakage.'"

4

I walked by the building at Pikk 59 slowly. I was across the street and trying not to stare. It was five or six stories high, a nice enough building overall. I stopped, tied my shoe, and looked over.

A man walked by me when I stood up, and I guess I hadn't been as inconspicuous in my reconnoitering as I had thought, because he slowed and half whispered, "Tallest building in Estonia, you know,"

I shrugged.

"Even from the basement, you can see all the way to Siberia," he said. Then he tipped his cap and resumed walking.

I walked away in the same direction. Two blocks down, I entered a corner store and bought two tins of tomato soup and a few small rolls. Dinner. Then me and my little paper bag retraced my route — except, the second time, I walked on the same side of the street as the NKVD/MVD/Whatever-the-hell headquarters.

Christ, they were all the same. The one in Cologne was like that when the Gestapo ran it before the war, as was the one in Lyon during the war, as was the one run by the Hungarian secret police in Budapest after the war. All the same — nondescript, nice enough, but all with a purpose.

The cells were always in the basement, and I could see that it was true at Pikk 59, too. But there was a twist. In the rest — but especially in Cologne — the windows at ground level gave away many of the secrets. They were the high windows at the top of the basement cells and, in Cologne, they were barred but without glass. That meant you could always hear the screams. It also meant, in the summertime, you could smell the shit from the buckets provided to the prisoners.

But it was different at Pikk 59. The windows at ground level were all bricked up. You couldn't hear anything, and you couldn't smell anything. And if the man on the street knew what went on inside — that you could see all the way to Siberia from the basement — there was still a desire for at least a hint of discretion. Not that it really mattered. I mean, torture was torture.

As I walked along, I heard a shout from above and stopped and stared. On the tower above the church next door, St. Olaf's, there were two soldiers standing on a landing area at the base of the spire, holding ropes that were somehow attached to a third soldier who was rappelling up to the top, to the cross. Or, rather, he was rappelling down and then stopping. He was holding what appeared to be a wire, and I looked up and saw that it was attached to an antenna that shared the summit of the spire with the cross.

The soldier yelled again. I thought he said, "Loose connection." I watched him fiddle with the wire and a pair of pliers for maybe 20 seconds, and then he waved and shouted something else, and then his compatriots gradually let out some slack in the ropes and the soldier made his way down.

So, they used the church as a radio station. If it wasn't the tallest building in Tallinn, it was among them. My guess was that there was a virtually unobstructed view in every direction, all the way to the horizon — good for sending messages and good for intercepting them, too. Maybe Gerhard Grimm and his radio prohibition weren't as stupid as I had thought. I mean, I still thought he was a Nazi but maybe he wasn't an idiot.

Nazis. I kind of wondered what my co-workers at the vodka warehouse thought of me. Because I only spoke enough Estonian to get by, I would never be able to qualify as a local, or anything close to a local. So the cover story Fritz Ritter concocted for me was that of a German soldier who deserted from the Wehrmacht during the war for the time-honored reason: I fell in love with a girl from the hinterlands and got her pregnant. I told the story the same way every time, as recently as the previous week when Ruubert, the bottle-return guy, cornered me in the bar.

"Her father hated me, and her two brothers hated me even more," I said. "But what were they going to do? I don't know if I loved her, but I was willing to do the honorable thing. We lived in an out-building on the farm, a shithole that I tried to fix up as best I could. I worked on the farm — potatoes — and we settled in, but then the baby came early and Riina died during the childbirth. She was dead before the doctor ever got there. They both were dead. And, well, the fucking father and two fucking brothers didn't give me time to grieve, if you know what I mean. We buried them on a Monday morning, and they kicked me out of there by Monday night, and even if they hadn't forced me, I would have been gone the next day. I didn't know what to do, or where to go, or how to take the next step in my life. So, I came to Tallinn."

People seemed to buy the story. Dead wife, dead baby — that kind of story naturally discouraged a lot of follow-up questions. Ruubert, though, did pick at the one loose thread.

"You? In the army? How old are you?"

"I was 40 in 1943, when they scooped me up," I said, knocking off a couple of years. "Like, literally — right off of the street between deliveries. Single man, working as a messenger in Berlin — those were good enough qualifications by then. I mean, Stalingrad..."

Dead wife, dead baby, Stalingrad — they all tended to stop the interrogation. Nobody wanted to think about the first two for any longer than was necessary, and everybody understood the last one. Saying "Stalingrad" in the years after the second war was like saying "Verdun" in the years after the first war. They both were shorthand for "hell," and everybody who had ever put on a uniform got it immediately.

Ruubert did say, "Were you th—"

Was I there? There at Stalingrad? I interrupted him before he got it out, even as I wasn't sure he was going to manage it.

"Let's not talk about it," I said. Then I looked down. I hoped it wasn't too theatrical, but it turned out to be just right.

Ruubert punched me on the shoulder, and then he reached over and poured for both of us from one of the bootleg bottles the bar allowed us to bring in. If we agreed to purchase one drink apiece, and left two bottles as a gratuity, they let us drink our own stuff and stay all night.

"To better days," Ruubert said, and we both emptied our glasses in one gulp. And with that, he joined the list of co-workers who bought my story and felt sorry for me. It worked exactly as Fritz said it would. In my heart, I knew it would. I had, after all, lost a wife and an unborn child years earlier, and knew the effect of telling the story. And then it hit me for a second. It had been years since I told the complete story to anyone. And even when I did tell it, or even think about it, I concentrated on the plane crash Manon died in near the English Channel, the plane crash fleeing the Gestapo in France. I almost never mentioned our unborn child anymore.

Still, before I left on the mission, I expressed my typical skepticism and presented Fritz with a list of what-ifs. Including, "What if somebody asks me the baby's name?"

"Then you make one up," he said. "Or, better yet, you put your hand over your brow, and look down, and shield your eyes, and start to say something, and then you stop and croak out, 'I'm sorry. I can't. I just can't.' But it will never get that far. If it does, I'll double your salary for a month."

And he was right. It never got close to that far.

I allowed myself to stare at the soldiers working on the spire for maybe 20 seconds because, well, it was a natural enough reaction for a passer-by. But when I was done with my gawking, I walked quickly past the NKVD headquarters. Two other things struck me, though, even as I pretty much stared at my shoes as I walked. First, that there was no guard on the outside of the front door. Second, that there was a single soldier posted in the alley next to the building.

5

_____

Linna was naked on the couch when I walked into my apartment. The time before, she had been naked in the kitchen, leaning over to grab something from a lower cabinet — my favorite pose. The time before that, she had been toweling off after a shower.

"What's for dinner?" she asked.

"Soup and bread," I said, as evenly as I could, as if I had been expecting her.

"Peasant food."

I shrugged.

"Come over here, peasant," she said, holding out her hand for me to grasp. She took charge immediately, as she had done the previous two times. Boss-and-employee seemed to be our relationship, clothed or otherwise.

We were drunk the first time and arrived together. The next morning, she woke up first and was dressing when I finally stirred.

"It goes without saying…" she said.

"…that this will go without saying," I said.

"Exactly."

She left for work first. I followed by a half-hour, enjoying a long, hot shower and a long, hot remembrance of the night before. This was an incredible woman, and it seemed clear that the sex would be the best kind of sex — the kind without strings attached. Amoral, apolitical, great ass — with Linna, all the A's were covered. Clearly, she also had the ability to pick a lock, seeing as how I never gave her a key to the apartment.

Three surprise visits, maybe two weeks apart, and they were all essentially the same: sex, eat, exit. After the first night, she never stayed over again. We never talked about it at work. She treated me in the same way she treated the rest of the employees — like shit when I screwed something up, like a big brother when I did my job. If anyone in the warehouse had any idea that we were sleeping together, I would be shocked. Half of the time, I had to remind myself — although when I got a look at that ass when she was walking away from me, well, my hormones took care of the reminding just fine.

So, that night — after I had done my reconnoitering at Pikk 59 — was like the others had been: sex, soup, see ya. At work the next day, I arrived to a ruckus whose origin I had trouble deciphering. All I knew was that there was a problem with a shipment of potatoes, and that Linna was alternately hissing directly at Artur in his little office — like, nose-to-nose — and then bellowing generally into the vast expanse of the warehouse. It was a big space, and discretion suggested to all of the workers simultaneously that the place to be at that particular moment was nowhere near Linna. I sat in one of the trucks, absent-mindedly checking the delivery paperwork for the rest of the week and tuning out the yelling — although certain phrases still registered. "That thieving motherfucker" was one that she repeated at least three times.

I had my head in the drivers' schedules when I heard Linna yelling my name on an endless loop.

"Alex!"

"Alex!"

"Alex!"

Each was louder than the previous one, and the fourth one was accompanied by Linna banging on the rolled-up window of the truck's cab.

"You're going to have to change those fucking things," she said, pointing at the delivery schedules.

"To what?"

"Clear your day for next Tuesday, and clear the van of all deliveries," she said. "You've got to drive me someplace."

"All day?"

"All fucking day," she said. She turned and walked away, which was my favorite view, even as Linna yelled again, "That thieving motherfucker."

6

The more I thought about it, it seemed to me that the best way to get inside the NKVD/MVD/Whatever-the-hell headquarters was to do it legitimately. And, no, not to get my ass arrested and detained in one of the basement cells with the bricked-over windows. That would have been legitimate but crazy. Another way seemed obvious, once I thought about it.

The headquarters was an office building, basically — and every office building needed to be cleaned on a daily-to-weekly basis. I didn't imagine that NKVD agents, even with their obvious security concerns, debased themselves by mopping their own floors, and dusting their own desks, and changing their own light bulbs, and cleaning their own toilets. If I had to guess, they were like every other office building in Tallinn. That is, they hired a cleaning crew from a service. In the case of the Soviet secret police, they would take care of any security concerns among the workers the old-fashioned way — by scaring the hell out of all of them if so much as a paper clip was found to be out of place when they were finished, and if so much as a pencil eraser was found in one of the cleaner's pockets when they were searched at the end of their shift.

So, the way I figured it, my best way in would be to get hired onto the cleaning crew — which meant I had to figure out the name of the cleaning company and then go from there. That was why I was parked in the front window of a little restaurant called Lulu's for the third time in a week, working my way through the menu, allowing the ancient waitress to mother me when I told her the fiction about my dead wife and baby. Her definition of mothering was a free order of rice pudding and a free coffee refill after dessert, and that was fine with me. She delivered them with a wink, and a smile, and a light pat on my shoulder.

The front window offered a decent vantage point of the headquarters building. It wasn't perfect because it was down the street, but it was okay. I could see the front door, and I could see the entrance of the alley on the far side, and it was the best I was going to do. It wasn't as if I could afford to be seen hanging out in front of the building all day. Even a series of walk-bys would create a real risk of being noticed. I mean, the people who worked inside were cops and spies, after all.

In the six-or-so hours I was in the front window at Lulu's, six hours over three nights, I never saw anything resembling a cleaning crew that pulled up to the front door. I never saw a delivery of any kind. Individual men and pairs of men came in and out on a fairly regular basis, but that was it — and they were all wearing suits or trench coats.

On two of the nights, though, I did see a small van drive into the alley between 6.30 and 7. Of course, I had no idea what it was and no way of telling from the restaurant. There were other buildings in there, other back doors that opened onto the alley. I didn't count, but there had to be at least four, and maybe six, buildings that backed onto the alley. The van could have been a delivery vehicle of some kind. It could have been taking a short cut to the next street. It could have been anything. And besides not knowing what the van contained, I had no idea when it left because it must have driven away out of the other end of the alley. At least, the second time I saw the van, the alley was empty — other than the single soldier — 10 minutes later, which was about as quick as I could pay the bill and walk down the street to see.

I decided to stick with it for a couple of more nights, working my way down the Lulu's menu. The first, no van arrived. But the second, just before 7 p.m., it pulled into the alley. This time, I had paid my bill earlier and was nursing the coffee. So, as soon as I saw the van, I was out on the street.

When I walked by, I saw the van parked in the alley, in a little nook maybe 50 feet from the back door that the soldier was guarding. I looked closer, and there were at least three doors that might have made sense as a destination for whomever had been in the van. I just couldn't tell. Then there was the problem of the van being unmarked, which meant if it was a cleaning crew, the name of the company wasn't stenciled on the side. Without that name, I had no way of worming my way in.

I stopped and tied my shoe and peered down the alley from across the street. There was the soldier, leaning against the wall, gun at his side, as bored as any soldier in any army at any time in recorded history would likely be in the same circumstance. There was the van, maybe 50 feet from the soldier, empty. I scanned the back for any kind of marking — on the doors, on the bumper, anywhere — but there was nothing.

I stood up and brushed off my knee and walked away. The only thing of which I was certain as I left Pikk Street was that I was going to need another plan.

7

The drive to Tartu with Linna took a couple of hours. As it turned out, the thieving motherfucker was her cousin, Valter. The shorthand version of the tale was that Valter was one of Linna's main potato suppliers and he was unilaterally attempting to change the financial terms of their arrangement six months before they were due for a renegotiation. He was withholding delivery of five truckloads of potatoes — "a fucking shipment for which he has already been fucking paid, the motherfucker," Linna explained.

She worked herself into a state as she explained it all, then calmed herself. She might have been furious, but this was business. When we arrived at the farm, Linna and Valter said their hellos but did not hug or shake hands. Linna and Valter's wife, Rahne, did hug, though. And we all sat down in the front room and ate sandwiches from plates on our laps, the awkward silences filled mostly by me telling my fictional backstory.

Then, after his last bite, Valter said, "Give me two minutes to explain before you bite my head off." Linna nodded.

As fast as he could, Valter talked of the evils of the collectivization that the Soviets had forced on the Estonian farmers, and how much it had cost him, and the unfairness of the quotas that the government put on his farm, and how he had worked out a way to keep supplying Linna on the sly, but that it was tenuous.

Just then a kid walked into the room, leaned over and kissed his mother.

"It was his idea," Valter said. "If it works, it will more than pay for the tuition."

The kid hugged Linna and then stuck out his hand to me. Rikkart was 20 years old, in his third year at the university in Tartu. He was home, Rahne said, to get a good meal and to have his laundry done. She was beaming when she said it.

Rikkart sat down and listened to his father sing his praises by describing the scheme. During the collectivization process, each farmer had a meeting with the local land agent in order to determine the arable acreage of his property. That determined the production quota.

"The key was always going to be the map," Valter said.

"And I knew someone at school who was a draftsman," Rikkart said.

"And I was able to obtain a copy of our map," Valter said.

"From Vincenc, the land agent," Rikkart said.

"Who was, uh, amenable," Valter said, "amenable" being the euphemism for "bribe-able."

The way Valter explained it, there was a forest that abutted on one portion of his property, and a small mountain whose foothills were adjacent on the other side. Their friendly draftsman was able to draw a new map where the forest was a few acres bigger than on the original, and the foothills encroached on the other side by a few acres more than was true.

"It was really a beautiful job, and the kid pretty much did it for beer money," Valter said. "Vincenc put the new map in the files, and it now lists my farmable land as about 82 percent of the truth, and the rest is where your shipments come from."

"So, what's the problem?" Linna said.

"Vincenc has a shadow on his lung — they did the X-ray in Tallinn."

Valter stopped talking. I looked at Linna.

"So, bad?" she said.

"He's already stopped working," Valter said.

"So, a replacement land agent takes over," she said. "And you just have to deal with it. So, what's his name?"

"The new man? Not important," Valter said.

"So, what is important? You have the maps," Linna said.

"The maps are good and there's a chance they'll work forever," Valter said. "As long as the new agent is…"

"Amenable?" I said.

"Amenable, yes, or at least uninterested," Valter said. "The problem is that the likely replacement agent is…"

Valter's voice trailed off. Rahne got up to leave the room. We all were left looking at each other.

"Tell them," Rikkart said.

Valter waved his hand.

"I can't believe I told you," Valter said.

"Well, they should know exactly what we're dealing with," Rikkart said, and then he picked up where his father couldn't, or wouldn't. As he began to speak, Valter left the room to join his wife.

"Pop was screwing the guy's sister," Rikkart said.

"Recently?" Linna said.

"No, long time ago," Rikkart said. "Before I was born."

"But after your parents were married?"

"Unclear," he said. "It's the question he won't answer, and the question I don't want to press him on. In some ways, I can't believe he told me everything he did."

Rikkart stopped, and took a breath, and then started laughing.

"I mean, it was a hell of a line," he said. "Pop was in the bar with this guy, and it sounds like they were pretty far gone. And the guy accused Pop of fucking his sister, and Pop was drunk enough that he admitted it. Except, well, he admitted it rather colorfully."

Rikkart stopped. I said, "Colorfully?"

"As in, 'She has swallowed so many of my children that she likely would have been able to shit out a regiment of the Red Army,'" Rikkart said.

"Colorful is one word for it," I said.

"Needless to say, that was the last drink they shared," Rikkart said. "And other than the occasional, awkward meeting in a store or on the street, they have pretty successfully avoided each other over the years. It isn't that easy to do in a place like Tartu, but they've managed. I mean, he only told me fairly recently, but it now explains why there were certain restaurants we never ate in when I was a kid. But anyway, if Toomas becomes the land agent..."

"That's his name?" I said.

"Yeah, Toomas," he said.

"But, well, fuck Toomas. I mean, you still have the maps," Linna said.

"We do, and they will hold up under many circumstances — it's not like they're bringing in surveyors or anything," Rikkart said.

"So, what's the problem?" Linna said.

"The neighbors," he said. "If you put their maps side-by-side with our maps, the changes will be obvious — it's the same forest on the one side, the same foothills on the other. Theirs would be accurate, ours wouldn't be. Now, you'd have to have a reason to check the maps against each other, and, well..."

"It might take a regiment of the Red Army to restrain the new agent's desire to find some way to finally get back at your father?" I said.

"That's the concern," Rikkart said.

"All over some 20-year-old blowjobs," Linna said.

"Not the blowjobs," I said.

"Rubbing his nose in the blowjobs," Rikkart said.

"So to speak," I said, and even Linna laughed.

"Pop needs the financial cushion," Rikkart said. He was talking directly to Linna at that point. "The collective, it's a terrible living. He needs what he makes from you on the side. And so, he needs extra cash now in case the maps get discovered. He also needs it in case he can find a way to pay off the new land agent. Either way, that's it. He's just trying to find a way to survive."

Linna got up and went through the door that Valter and Rahne had left through. Five minutes later, she was back.

"He's getting three-quarters of what he demanded, effective immediately," she said, and then she headed for the front door.

As she reached for knob, she turned back and said, "Men are such idiots."

As the door opened, she turned again.

"But I have to admit, it was a hell of a line about the Red Army," Linna said. "I would have loved to see the guy's face when your father said it."

8

Linna took a nap for maybe half of the ride back to Tallinn. When she woke up, she began talking as if picking up a conversation that we had been having the whole time.

"I mean, there's just no long term," she said.

"No long-term what?"

"No long-term survival."

"We all die, Linna."

"I'm not talking about life and death," she said, adding the dismissive punctuation, "Christ."

"So, what then?"

"The business. The sale of bootleg vodka in the city of Tallinn and the immediate environs. We're fucking doomed."

"Doomed is a little harsh," I said. "I mean, I get that there are challenges. But you've dealt with challenges in the past, based on everything you and the rest of them have said. You've dealt with them, usually with an envelope stuffed with cash. I have to think that still works in whatever the circumstance."

Linna sighed in reply. Then she ran the fingers of both hands through her hair.

"The cash is not never-ending," she said.

"Based on what I see coming in, it isn't ending anytime soon."

"But it's more complicated than that."

"So, tell me," I said.

At which point, Linna again combed her hair with her fingers, and then took a deep breath, and then began talking. It was as if she was reading from a script. During her little nap, or maybe in the weeks and months before, she obviously had been practicing her arguments.

"The first problem is Valter's problem, the collectivization," she said. "That much is obvious, I would think — even to you."

"I'm hurt that you think so little of my intellect."

"Just shut up and listen."

Linna continued on. For the first few years, the Soviets were more babysitters than bosses, she said.

"They took some people and sent them to the gulags, but most of us, they pretty much left alone. They were just like an added layer of police assholes. They were after political enemies and old Nazis. Most of the rest of us, they just left us alone — even the illegal businesspeople like me. And, you're right — a fat envelope handed to a fat-fingered captain in a Red Army uniform took care of pretty much every problem. That way, we were all winners."

"And now?"

"They're not just babysitters anymore," she said. "They're absorbing us into the country, and they're bringing in a lot of their rules."

"Like the collectives," I said.

"Exactly. So, every farmer now has a production quota, stuff that he grows that goes to the state — and they're not all as smart as Valter and Rikkart, the college boy. My supply is getting squeezed. I have five farmers who supply me with potatoes, and it's already happening on the margins. It's just going to get worse. And without potatoes..."

"You're screwed," I said.

"So to speak," Linna said. "But it's worse than that. I mean, we could find a way to scrounge for what we needed for a while, I think. There are plenty of land agents with fat fingers, I have to believe. But there's something else now. Something worse."

"Worse than no potatoes?"

"Yes, worse."

Linna stopped, sighed, closed her eyes for a few seconds. She stayed quiet until I said, "So, are you going to tell me or not?"

One more sigh.

"It's like this," she said. "Let's just say that I have a police contact."

"Regular police?"

"Regular police. And let's say, I spend time with him on a fairly regular basis, and that there is drinking involved."

"Among other things," I said.

"Fuck you," she said.

"It wasn't a judgment."

"The hell it wasn't," she said, and then she waved her hand, waved the remark away.

"I do what needs to be done," Linna said. "And, well, my friend has told me that the pressure from the Soviets is increasing. They want the bootleg vodka business to end. As he told me the last time, 'They want us to squeeze the life out of you.'"

"But why?" I said.

"It's pretty simple," she said. "The sale of vodka in the authorized stores is the biggest source of revenue for the Soviets in the entire country."

"That doesn't seem possible."

"Well, it is. You've seen how much we sell."

"All we can make," I said.

"Exactly. And the overlords have been doing the math, and they've decided that the best, quickest way for them to increase their revenues — money they need to pay for all of the army and NKVD and the rest of them — is by putting me and the other bootleggers out of business."

"And forcing everyone to buy their vodka from the state-authorized stores, where they take a cut."

"Right," she said. "And, well, I don't know if Stalin has fat fingers or not, but I have no way to get an envelope to him, so I can't find out."

Linna went quiet again, and I did, too. The more I thought about it, the more I became convinced that she was right, that the business was doomed. Maybe not in two months, maybe not in two years — but if she was right, and the Soviets needed the money to pay for their occupation of the country, and if the orders were coming from Moscow, and if the ledgers were being examined in Moscow, Linna's enterprise was done for. The only remaining question was how long she would continue to run the risk of operating the illegal distillery, and what the penalty might be if her friend in the Tallinn police department was given no choice but to act. You'd like to think she had bought herself enough goodwill — from the cop, and the people across the parking lot at the NKVD prison, and the rest of the fat-fingered legion. You'd like to believe they would rescue her in a pinch, that they wouldn't allow her to have her safety endangered.

At the same time, though, Linna was pretty hard-headed when it came to the business. I couldn't help but wonder — not if she would hear the hints from the cop and the rest of them, but if she would listen to them. This was a woman who gave orders. She didn't take them — at least, not in my presence.

I looked over and she was sleeping, snoring softly. A bumpy stretch of road woke her up, but she remained quiet. It was only when we reached the outskirts of Tallinn when she finally spoke, just a couple of words.

"Your place, okay?" Linna said. I looked over, and her eyes were still closed.

9

The next morning, Linna wanted to walk — not to anyplace in particular, it seemed. She just said, "Come with me," and I did. It was the way of our relationship, if you could call it that. You have interactions with some people, and it works out that each of you has a role that never seems to change. I had a buddy in school, bigger and louder than me, and the relationship was defined early: he told the jokes, and I laughed at them, and that was it. And so, Linna and I each had our roles. She told me to sleep with her, and I did. She told me to go for a walk, and I did.

But we were just wandering — left here, right there, with no conversation between us. It had been that way since the ride from Tartu, pretty much. We undressed without talking and had sex without talking. We ate some food and then had sex again without talking. I tried at one point — "Hey, are you okay?" — and was met with a tired reply consisting of two words: "I'm fine." But she wasn't, and I really didn't know her well enough to be able to make an educated guess. I mean, the bootlegging business was about to be challenged, as she had explained, but it was only a business. This seemed bigger somehow, deeper.

After about 10 minutes of wandering around the Old Town, Linna steered us onto Vene Street. She stopped in front of the big building at No. 9 and pointed.

"The post office?" I said.

"Telegraaf House," she said, quietly.

"Same difference."

"Telegraaf House," she said, even quieter this time. "Telegraaf House. My father, he always insisted. He always said, 'The proper name for a proper landmark.'"

I had no reply. I had no idea what she was talking about, what brought up the topic. Linna crossed the street, and I followed her. She sat on the curb, and I sat next to her.

"He worked there," she said.

I nodded.

"It really was the nerve center of the city, maybe the country. The main post office. The hub of all of the telegraph lines. And the telephones. If you wanted to make a phone call before the war, this is where you came. People didn't have phones in their homes then — well, not normal people. You came here. And my father, he designed a lot of it. He was so proud of it. If anybody asked what he did for a living, he would always say, 'I give people the world.'"

She looked at me, and I hoped that my face showed a combination of interest and sympathy and mystery, because those were the things I was feeling. We locked eyes for a second, and then she said, "The bombers came in 1944, March of 1944, March 9."

"Germans?" I said.

"Soviets," she said. And then her eyes dropped, and Linna was staring into the gutter when she whispered, "Fuckers."

My inclination was to put my arm around her, or to grab for her hand, to comfort her physically, but I resisted it. The silence hung there for maybe 10 seconds, and her eyes never left the gutter, and then she started talking again.

"Incendiary bombs," Linna said. "Designed to burn the place to the ground. Fuckers. And the thing was, we kind of knew they were coming, and the rest of my family stayed home, but not Papa. No, he had to go to work, to his beloved Telegraaf House. My mother tried to talk him out of it, but he said, 'It's more important than ever to keep the lines open, to make sure the world can see.' That's the last thing I heard him say."

"So, it was hit?" A stupid thing to say, but the silences were becoming beyond uncomfortable.

"Doesn't look like it, does it?" Linna said. "But yeah, it was hit over on the far side. Didn't burn down, obviously. And the lines remained open the whole time. It was the last thing he said, when they found him. He asked one of his co-workers, 'Still in good order, right?'"

"Where..."

"On the toilet," she said. "My Papa died on the fucking toilet at the fucking Telegraaf House because the fucking Russians decided to punish the citizens of Tallinn. And why, pray tell? What was our crime? We had the nerve to be overrun by the fucking Nazis."

This time, I did reach out my arm and put it over her shoulder. It remained there for about a second before Linna shrugged it off and then stood up.

"Come on," she said, and I followed her back to my place and then to work. She sat in her office, and I did my deliveries, and we didn't talk again, not properly, for days.

10

The small delivery van — the one that I had driven to Tartu with Linna — had an off-the-books function for many of the workers, one joked about in whispers. It wasn't that Linna would necessarily object, but it wasn't something a lot of the guys wanted to banter about, especially the married guys. When I was given custody of the keys, it was as if I had become the priest who was governed by the seal of the confessional. So, when somebody asked, it was almost always a surreptitious approach and a quick question:

"Anybody using the Fuck Truck tonight?"

There was a small rolled-up mattress that was shoved into one of the back corners of the cargo area, camouflaged by an empty crate or two — and, well, so much for the amenities. But if one of the men happened to find himself in a temporary relationship, and either his or the woman's bedroom was otherwise occupied — spouse, boyfriend, nosy roommate, whatever — the Fuck Truck was a valuable off-the-books fringe benefit for employees, more valuable in its own way than the free vodka.

The demand apparently grew as the temperature dropped. As it was, I was being asked about three times a week for the keys. That day, it was Branko, one of the distillers, who shuffled over after a trip to the toilets to ask the question:

"Anybody using the Fuck Truck tonight?"

"Sorry, Branko — you're too late. It's spoken for."

"Christ. I bet it's that asshole Vladdy. Fucking Vladdy."

"My lips are sealed," I said.

"You don't need to tell me. I know. I mean, I fucking know. He was all over that Ana at the bar the other night. I fucking know. You know Ana, right?"

"Blonde hair, tiny ass?"

"That's her," Branko said. "Blonde hair, tiny ass, always available. I've had her in the Fuck Truck, you know. I know at least two others, too."

"One more, and I think the law says we're going to have to put her name on the registration papers," I said.

"Fucking Vladdy."

"I didn't say anything." Branko waved away my denial.

"Fucking Vladdy. So, tomorrow night?"

"Wide open, so to speak," I said.

I had been hoping that no one would know that I was the one taking the van that night, and while silence would have been best, the Fucking Vladdy business would do — unless, of course, Vladdy and Branko were in the bar together. But, well, whatever. If worse came to worse, I could tell Branko that I was the one who needed the Fuck Truck, and I would permit him to believe that it was for the conventional off-the-books reason, not for the task I had fashioned.

Anyway, it was about 11 p.m. when I pulled the van into the alley next to the NKVD/MVD/Whatever-the-hell headquarters building. As it had been every time I had passed by on my surveillance rounds, the only human in the alley was the single soldier guarding the side door. As I passed him and parked, he perked up from what must have been a near nap. He actually seemed a bit startled.

"What's up friend?" I said.

"Who the hell are you?"

As I approached, the soldier noticed the precious cargo I was carrying — two bottles of our best bootleg vodka.

"What's this?"

"You ever work over at the prison?"

"Sometimes."

"Well, you know about our distillery, then."

"Across the parking lot?"

"Exactly," I said. "And, well, you're probably aware that we have an arrangement with your bosses at the prison. And, well, my boss was talking to your boss, and she—"

"Your boss is a she?"

"Smartest she you ever met."

"I don't care if they're smart, if you know what I mean," the soldier said. By that point, he had propped his rifle against the building and, with his two hands in front of him — as if resting on the hips of one of his not-smart favorites — began thrusting his pelvis rhythmically.

"Well, I guess brains can be overrated."

"Fucking right."

"Anyway, my boss and your boss were talking, and they decided that you guys working out here deserved a taste. So, they sent me over and, well, here."

The guy had stopped thrusting, and he took the two bottles and admired them in the moonlight. Then he said, "But there's another guy inside, working the front desk."

It was as I had expected, then. Two soldiers wouldn't be a problem.

"I have a couple more," I said. "Go get him."

I went back to the truck and pulled out two more of the

bottles I had prepared, along with one more for myself. Within a few seconds, the first soldier was accompanied by a second. I handed him two bottles, and unlike the first guy, the inside cat said thank you.

At which point, I opened my bottle, and they opened the first of their bottles, and the three of us proceed to stand in the alley, leaning against the wall, and drinking. I had spoken to the first guy in broken Estonian, but after a few swigs, we somehow settled on English as a way of communicating. In a sense, it didn't really matter, because soldiers were always keen to know the names of the various parts of the female anatomy in every language relevant to their service, and probably a few others. So, as I told them a World War I story involving me, my friend Leon, three overweight Italian girls from near Caporetto, and a jar of honey, it was clear that the language didn't really matter much. I could have offered Leon's refrain from that night — which he still repeated three decades later, if properly lubricated — in Swahili, and the two Soviet soldiers in the alley would have roared just the same. That said, I had no idea how to translate "sweet, sweet pussy" into Swahili.

The two of them were more than half-done with their first bottles. I never stopped being amazed and impressed by Russians' ability to put away vodka. They were terrible with wine and other spirits, but vodka for them really was in a different category. In the end, it kicked their asses like every-thing else in the alcohol family, but with vodka, it seemed to take longer. And well, that I was drinking water that night was my little secret.

When they stopped laughing at my tale, the inside cat began to tell his own dirty story. It involved him, three buddies, one girl from Riga, the girl's mother, and the little brother who stole their uniforms and then ransomed them back to the soldiers, one garment at a time. The inside guard was halfway through his recitation of the negotiations — with the little brother repeatedly saying, arms folded in front of him, "You think it's free to fuck my mother? What do you think this is?" — when he started to slur, and then to sink lower and lower, his back still against the wall of the building. The other soldier was already seated and asleep. The inside guy seemed to have a sense that something wasn't right, but it was just a quick flash on his face before he, too, was asleep.

That I had drugged their vodka bottles was also my little secret. I was wearing a black watch cap and eyeglasses with clear glass for lenses, and I adjusted the glasses because they felt so unfamiliar on my face. Then I checked my watch. It was 11.30.

11

The pistol with the silencer was jammed into my inside coat pocket. It was a small revolver, enough to stun a man but not kill him unless it was fired directly into his head or his heart. I had French Resistance friends who would have sneered when they saw it.

"Woman's gun," they would say, with a sad shake of their head. "For after they get their nails painted."

The silencing contraption nearly doubled its size, and only the padding in the coat concealed it. Not that hiding it mattered all that much once I had left my two friends sleeping in the alley. If I got accosted inside, well, I wasn't disguised and I didn't have any kind of plausible story. If that happened, accessibility to the gun was all that would matter.

Inside the building, the first hallway was dim, not dark. It ended in the reception area, also dim but with a pool of light over the front desk where the inside soldier had likely sat. It was a small space, all things considered, with a big staircase going up and a wide door through which I could see stairs leading down. That was, no doubt, where the cells were. That I would be avoiding that area went without saying. I had seen the cells in

Cologne and Lyon, and seen the stairs in Budapest, and that was plenty, thanks. I still had a recurring nightmare about electrodes being attached to my balls, and I didn't need my monthly terror to become daily again. Besides, down the stairs was where the rest of the guards were — although it was probably only one or two, and the likelihood was that he/they were either playing cards to stay awake or snoozing with a newspaper shielding their eyes from the overhead lights.

In any case, I was headed up the stairs to offices that I hoped were empty. That was where the administrators worked, without doubt — and given the proclivities of every military organization, well, let's say that for every NKVD torturer on the payroll, there were probably two pencil-pushers documenting and/or bitching about the soaring costs of rubber hoses and finger loppers.

At the top of the steps, I saw that the hallway on that floor was darker than the rest — but I could still navigate fine. I wasn't sure what I was looking for, but I hoped I might recognize a decent prospect for investigation when I saw it. Grimm had told me he wanted names of agents and work schedules and things like that, so I was looking for filing cabinets when I opened the first office door. What I saw, instead, was what appeared to be a big boss's office suite — a secretary's desk out front and then an inner office that seemed too plush for someone who actually worked for a living.

The second door I opened, though, was clearly what I needed. On the wall, a half-dozen clipboards hung on the wall in an even row. They were labeled by day — Monday to Friday, and Weekend. Six clipboards, each holding two sheets of paper, two lists of names. This was it. I could be in and out in less than five minutes — a dozen snapshots with the little camera in my pocket and out.

I was reaching for the first clipboard when I heard someone

on the staircase — not footsteps but whistling. Fuck. At least, I hadn't yet switched on the desk lamp. I left the clipboard where it was and, as quickly and quietly as I could manage, opened the office closet door and slipped inside. It was full of stacked cardboard boxes, but I managed to pretzel myself into place, and it wasn't that bad, except for the corner of the box jabbing into my ass.

The whistling got louder, and then the door of my office swung open. Damn. I couldn't see anything, other than the light that was switched on through the door's bottom crack. I couldn't see, but I could hear the guy sitting in the chair, and then I could hear the phone being dialed. Damn. Damn.

And then it got, well...

"Hi, baby. How's it going?"

Silence.

"You know, honey."

Silence.

"Maybe five minutes. He thinks I'm on the toilet."

Zipper unzipping.

"You know I do, baby."

Spitting sound.

"Tell me."

Chair squeaks.

"It's so fucking big."

Rhythmic squeaking.

"Now, do the thing."

More squeaking.

"No, the other hand."

Squeaking. Grunting.

"Ohbabyfuckbaby..."

Long silence.

Drawer opening.

Rustling, then silence.

"Oh, baby, I can't wait for Friday."

Phone hangs up.

Zipper zips.

Door opens and closes.

Whistling.

I waited for about a minute and then opened the closet door. The office smelled like sex. Christ. I switched on the desk lamp and looked at the first clipboard. It was a duty roster — names, ranks, work schedules. If it wasn't everything Grimm wanted, it would have to be enough.

The camera worked as it should — although I wouldn't know for sure until the film was developed, and I wasn't doing the developing. That would be Grimm's problem — and if the camera was a piece of junk, oh well. I mean, it wasn't as if I was going to be able to get back in a second time. I thought about taking the originals, but that was the last thing anybody needed — the NKVD/MVD knowing their stuff had been stolen. The camera would just have to work.

It really didn't take five minutes. I listened at the door for a minute before opening it and heard nothing. I crept into the dark hallway, and then down the steps, and then through the reception area. No one saw me. I was down the final hallway and to the door that opened onto the alley, and then I stopped and took a very long, very deep breath. Damn.

12

I had managed to avoid thinking about what would happen when I opened the door that led to the alley, but I always knew. I had glossed over it during the planning stages, but I always knew. I fixated on the smaller details, and about getting them to be as perfect as I could. I had tested the camera and had the film developed at a drugstore, trying different levels of lighting to see the minimum needed. I had gone out into the country and fired the gun with the silencer attached, to check not only the aim but also the sound. I had gone to an optician for the eyeglasses with the plain lenses, saying they were for a part in a play. At the chemist, I had explained my sleeping problems and had him explain what might happen if I accidentally overdosed the potion he had concocted for me. I had gone over all of those little details, and satisfied myself that they were as good as they could be, and fixated on them as I ran the operation over and over in my head.

But I always knew. And when I opened the door that led to the alley, my two little toy soldiers were still passed out on the ground, their bottles lying next to them — two still full, two empty and toppled, one of the empties broken.

I reached into the inner pocket of my coat and fingered the revolver. There was no other way, and... fucking Grimm. I blamed him. I blamed him for the assignment, and for what was about to happen. For what had to happen.

The two saps, splayed out on the cinders, had done nothing wrong. They did not deserve what was about to happen. They had survived the war and were now tending to a backwater. They had likely seen combat, and made it out the other side, and were posted to a quiet place where their chief concerns were likely frozen vodka and warm breasts — in whatever order. This shouldn't be happening, but it was — all for a few lists of names and work hours. Fucking Grimm.

There was really no way around it. If I had managed to get myself assigned to the cleaning crew, I would have been able to pull it off — but that wasn't happening. There was no way to work the surveillance in order to find out who was supplying the crew. It just wasn't possible. And this plan, well, it was the next best thing. In truth, it was probably the only possible thing — and it worked. It worked fucking beautifully. I wasn't inside for 15 minutes, and it would have been less than 10 if not for the guard's dirty phone call. In, out, mission accomplished.

I took the gun out of my pocket and looked at it, always a bit surprised at the size of the silencer. I just stared at it for a second, holding it in my right hand, my finger behind the trigger guard. Fucking Grimm.

I had considered just leaving the two of them in the alley to be found by their morning replacements, but I couldn't. It was just stupid. It was malpractice, and it could have gotten me killed. Because, while I fooled around with the hat and the eyeglasses, I had known all along that it didn't really matter if the two of them recognized me or not. The problem was the story about the vodka. There had been no getting around that part. They needed to believe I had been sent by the bosses at the prison to deliver my little gift, and that was that. If the two of them had been awake in the morning, they would have remembered the van and they would have remembered the story. Hat, eyeglasses, bullshit. None of that mattered. They NKVD would have crossed the parking lot and raided the distillery before lunchtime. And even if I had somehow been able to convince their bosses that these two Soviet soldiers, experienced vodka drinkers, had passed out in the alley after drinking what they probably drank every Saturday night, the bosses knew that they hadn't sent me to deliver the bottles along with their best wishes. No, there was no way around it.

As my buddy Leon once told me, "Sometimes when you're fucked, the only way to unfuck yourself is to fuck somebody else."

"You think that up all by yourself?"

"No, I think it's in the Old Testament somewhere," Leon said. "Maybe Wisdom. No, probably Proverbs."

And that's what was going through my head when I held the pistol to the temple of the outside soldier, and fired once. And then, to the head of the inside soldier, the same thing.

You could smell the gunshots, but the silencer really did its job. It was like two thuds more than two bangs, neither of them much louder than if I had hit the two of them on the ass with a two-by-four. Whack. Whack.

Still, I was scared. I stayed crouched over the bodies and listened, but I heard nothing. I stole a look down either end of the alley — to my left, and my right, and my left again. Nothing. All quiet.

I looked down and managed to hop out of the way of the blood pooling near my feet. I picked up the two full bottles, and the one empty bottle, and the other bottle that had broken into three neat pieces, and put them in the back of the van. Then I turned the bodies and removed the wallets from the back pockets, taking the money and tossing what was left onto the cinders. Then I undid their pants and yanked them down. Finally, I pissed on the spilled vodka puddle, just to camouflage it a bit, not that it mattered. After coming upon the scene in the morning, the cinders would be dry and the NKVD/MVD/Whatever-the-hell would probably spend the upcoming days preoccupied with questioning every hooker in Tallinn — female, male, whatever. Pants down, wallets empty — what else could it be but thieving hookers? And with any luck, that would be that.

13

Two nights later, I jammed the roll of film into my pocket and got on Antti's boat for a trip to Helsinki. Antti and I, the film and my guilt — it was a crowded crossing of the gulf. Antti sensed my preoccupation immediately.

"What's the problem, baby?" he said.

"Baby? I thought you said I'm almost as old as you are."

"You are. It's just a figure of speech."

"Well, fuck your figure of speech."

"Fine. So, what's the problem, pussy?" he said.

I couldn't help but laugh. And seeing as how I had confided in the Ancient Mariner on the previous crossing, I figured, what the hell. I really wasn't risking anything. If the NKVD/MVD/Whatever-the-hell arrested Antti and turned him, well, he didn't know anything about me in a personal sense. He didn't know my name, or where I lived in Tallinn. If he was going to get me arrested, it would happen the next time I booked passage on his floating piece of shit — and the details I had given him would have nothing to do with it.

So, I told him everything — about the assignment to get the

duty rosters from the headquarters building, and the cleaning crew business that I couldn't pull off, and the way I hid in the closet while the guard got busy on the telephone with his girlfriend.

"I wonder if that would work on the radio," Antti said, lifting the receiver from its cradle.

"You'd need a woman on the other end, old man."

"I've got women," he said. Then, after a pause, "Incoming."

That I was downwind from his latest masterpiece could be measured in the actual watering of my eyes, and a slight bit of gagging.

"Jesus Christ," I said.

"Cabbage for dinner. Sorry."

Antti paused again, and then said, "So, you got what you needed. What's the problem?"

I explained the problem, the two problems, the two innocent men who I left with bullets in their head in the alley. I painted the problem, and that I had no choice, and I punctuated it all with one "fucking Grimm" and one "goddamned Grimm."

Antti was quiet after I finished. The water was reasonably smooth, and the moon was hidden behind the clouds, which made it a relatively pleasant ride. I was done, Antti was done, and the boat just kind of skipped along.

And then he said, "A conscience."

I just looked at him.

"A conscience can be a dangerous thing," he said. And then he was quiet again, and then he started talking again.

"You know when the Russians came," he said.

"Which time?"

"Right. After the Nazis — that time. They bombed the city."

"Tallinn, right," I said, remembering Linna's story about Telegraaf House and her father. "In 1944."

"Right, in 1944. You know, it's always been a complicated place."

"Estonia?"

"Yeah, Estonia," Antti said. "First, the Russians. Then, the Nazis. Then, the Russians again. And every time there was a change, well, people are people. Human beings are human beings. You do what you have to do to get along, right? That's pretty much everybody. And while, well, we had people who resisted the Russians, and other people who resisted the Nazis, and other people who are resisting the Russians again today — but that wasn't most people. Most people..."

"Get along to go along," I said. It was a concept I understood completely. When I had been fighting in the Resistance in Paris, about 95 percent of the people in the city were keeping their head down and staring at their shoes when they walked on the street, just trying to get to the next day. It was human nature, and I got it even if it sometimes infuriated me.

"Get along to go along — I like that phrase," Antti said. "But there were others who were a little more enthusiastic in their attempt to get along. You know, the kinds who..."

"Sucked a little too much Nazi dick," I said.

"So to speak."

"And then, when the Soviets came in 1944..."

"The ones who had sucked too much Nazi dick were now worried that the Russians would jail them and torture them..."

"And feed them their own dicks," Antti said.

"So to speak."

"Anyway, those people needed to get out," he said. "And, well, my business was booming. And, well, they were mostly just weak people. You know, pathetic. Pathetic more than truly evil, and I was happy to take their money. And it was a lot of money. They paid whatever I charged. I was making three or four runs a week. But then, there was this one guy."

"What was his name?"

"Don't know," Antti said. "Like I don't know your name, baby. It's easier that way. But this one guy, he was just a total piece of shit. Not pathetic — evil. Truly evil. A true Nazi believer. Spouting off the whole way about killing Jews. He would say things like, 'Estonia is Jew-free. I did that.' Just a fucking monster. Talking about Hitler having a great vision, and how the counterattack would be coming any day, and how he would set up in Finland with some others and prepare for the next invasion. Just a delusional asshole, just going on and on. And after about an hour, I just couldn't take it anymore, money or no money."

I looked at Antti and he kind of pointed the palms of his hands toward the sky and shrugged.

"I shot him and threw him over the fucking side," he said. "And, well, once word got back that he didn't make it to Helsinki, let's just say that my business dried up a bit."

"A bit?"

"Completely," Antti said. "But it was even worse than that. Somebody talked to somebody, and suddenly I was hauled in by the NKVD. It was more of a courtesy torture than the full treatment. I was in the cells for two nights with no sleep and the lights on full, but that was it. They never touched me. And when I didn't give anything up, they let me go. I just knew they were watching me after that. Like, for years. All I could do was fish until they forgot about me."

"And you're sure they have, you know, forgotten about you?"

"Well, you're still alive, aren't you?" Antti said. "But the point of the story is, like I was saying: a conscience can be a dangerous thing."

In another half-hour, the boat was circling around to the back side of Suomenlinna. We passed the King's Gate, and then maneuvered into the little cove where Antti always dropped me off, the last 200 feet of the journey in a rubber dinghy so as to avoid the rocks on the shoreline.

"Let's see if you can keep dry this time," he said, as I was making my way down the rope ladder.

"Alex."

"What?"

"My name is Alex," I said, and then I began paddling toward the little beach.

14

_____

Gerhard Grimm was waiting in his customary place. I gave him the roll of film, and he gave me his customary ration of disdain.

I said, "I hope those names were worth it."

He said, "Worth what?"

"I had to kill two men to get them."

"I didn't tell you to kill anybody."

"You gave me an assignment, and it was the only way."

"Your failure of imagination is not my problem," Grimm said. At which point, the asshole folded his arms and waited for a reply. I had none, mostly because I had been cursing myself for the aforementioned failure of imagination, cursing myself since I pissed on the puddle of spilled vodka. And if I had come to the conclusion — drunk, sober, and in between — that there really had not been any other alternative, and that I had to stop beating myself up over it, I couldn't stop. Not yet, anyway.

"Well, is that it?" I said.

"Sit down."

"For what?"

"For your next fucking set of instructions," Grimm said. I

took a place next to him on the small boulder upon which he was perched, and then he got up and began pacing in front of me.

"The Forest Brothers," he said.

I didn't answer.

"You know about them, right?"

"Loved the Nazis, hated the Soviets, ran a bunch of hit-and-run attacks on the Soviets after they took over, hid in the forests between attacks."

"Close enough," Grimm said.

"What did I miss?"

"You were pretty much right, except for your tenses."

"Meaning?"

"You said 'hated' the Soviets, and you said 'hid' in the forests. Well, it isn't 'hated' — it's 'hate.' And it isn't 'hid' — it's hide."

"But I thought the Soviets cleaned them out, like, pretty recently," I said. "It was in the papers. It was right after I got here. They said they went into the forests and cleaned them out."

"First of all, what do you think they're going to say in the newspapers that they totally control?" Grimm said. "You think they're going to say that their clean-up operation was a failure?"

Grimm stopped, spat.

"Naive fucking idiot," he said.

"Now, listen—"

"No, you fucking listen. There were tens of thousands of them hiding in the woods. The Russkies got some of them, maybe most of them — but they didn't get them all, not nearly. And people who live out that way know that the Forest Brothers are still an issue for the Soviets in the hinterlands, still a pretty significant pain in their ass."

"Great — so what's that go to do with me?" I said.

"If you'd stop fucking interrupting—"

"Fine, fine, go right ahead, your fucking majesty."

"Just listen," Grimm said. "We need you to get one of the Forest Brothers out — need you to bring him here to me."

"No sweat. I'll just put in ad in the local paper."

"Don't be a dick."

"Don't be a fantasist," I said. "Just go into the woods and ask around until somebody leads me to the brother in question, and then kidnap him and bring him out and get him on a boat. No sweat. Are you fucking out of your mind?"

"You won't have to kidnap him," Grimm said. "He'll want to come once he's heard your spiel."

"Which is?"

"It's a simple message. You just need to tell him, 'Hansi Brugmann wants you back.'"

"And who the hell is Hansi Brugmann?"

"Brugmann was his commanding officer when the Germans were here," Grimm said. "They organized the locals who were willing to work for them, and they had German leaders. Hansi Brugmann was his CO, and he looked after him. Based on everything we know, he was beloved by his men, Brugmann was."

"Sounds fucking charming," I said.

"Well, they loved him. And Brugmann, he was next to his men — our Forest Brother included — shooting the Jews and passing the vodka bottle back and forth. Other people who got out said Brugmann always said, 'Don't ask the men to do something you wouldn't be willing to do yourself — except clean the latrines.'"

"Wait a minute," I said. "What are you talking about? Shooting the Jews? I mean, I know it happened in some places—"

"And Estonia was one of the places," Grimm said.

"But has that ever been—"

"Never. Never been reported on. Never been revealed, not to anyone."

"The Soviets don't know?"

"Now you're catching on," Grimm said. "The Jews came in on trains."

"From where?"

"Germany, Czech, wherever the fuck. They killed hundreds of them near a place called Kalevi. They had the Jews dig a big pit, and then Brugmann and his local helpers shot them and pushed them into the hole, and then they covered them up and planted saplings over the graves."

"And the Soviets don't know."

"And we want to keep it that way," Grimm said. "Look, this isn't my idea — it comes from way above my pay grade. But they think it's important to get all of the witnesses out, and based on the records we have captured, there were only eight of them. They're pretty sure that Tamm is the last one."

"Tamm?"

"Karl Tamm. The Forest Brother in question. We get him, the higher-ups tell me, and there's a good chance the secret of what's beneath the saplings leaves Estonia with him. And I don't think I need to tell you how the Soviets might use this against us if they knew, the propaganda value a story like that might have."

"Who gives a fuck?" I said. "We're suddenly worried that the Nazis are going to look back in the eyes of world opinion? And I'm supposed to risk my life to save their reputations? Fuck that. I'm out of here."

I stared hard at Grimm, trying to read his face, trying to see if my verbal shots at the Nazis were hitting him where he lived. I stood up, and I stared, but his face betrayed nothing. Then again, it was a pretty dark night.

"Sit the fuck down," Grimm said. "You still work for me. And even you're smart enough to see that this is complicated. It's not just the Germans' reputation we're talking about — it's the Estonians, too. We need the rest of the world to be at least a little sympathetic — to Germans trying to rebuild their society and to Estonians under Stalin's thumb. The sympathy is important. It will allow the German state to rebuild and it will keep the pressure on the Russians about these satellite states they have absorbed. Look, it's a big strategy with a lot of moving pieces, and I'm not even sure I understand it all. But, well, world opinion matters. And if everybody just thinks the whole lot of them are just a bunch of unrepentant Nazis..."

"Which a lot of them fucking are."

"Some, not a lot," Grimm said. "Like I said, it's complicated. Christ, you understand that. And Tamm, he's a potential embarrassment. He knows about Kalevi, where the bodies are buried, literally, and with saplings planted on top. And the Soviets can't be allowed to know about that, not if we can help it."

"But what about the leftover Nazi?" I said. "What did you call him? Hansi Brugmann?"

"It's all bullshit. It's true that Tamm loved him, along with the rest in his outfit. But Hansi hanged himself, like, two years ago in that prison."

"Patarei?"

"No, idiot," Grimm said. "Our prison — it's near Hamburg. I forget the name. But old Hansi hanged himself after he told our interrogators everything, including about Kalevi."

For the next half-hour, I picked away at Grimm, seeking details about the where and the how. I eventually told him that I was in, and then I headed back to the dinghy. As I rowed back to the boat, I wasn't sure if I had lied to him, though.

PART II

15

Part of me wanted to re-route Antti on the spot. I had enough cash with me to convince him to make a turn south toward Sweden, to have him take me there. I could find my way home to Vienna and just be fucking done with the whole thing.

Nazis. Old, unrepentant Nazis. It was what this always came back to, even a half-decade after Hitler ate his gun in the bunker — or, however he killed himself and Eva and the dog and the country.

I argued with Leon about them. I argued with my boss, Fritz Ritter, about them. That they both pretty much ended up in the same place would shock both of them, if they knew.

Fritz always argued in practicalities, saying that the worst of them have been killed or jailed and that the rest have been harnessed for the greater good — the fight against the Commies. Practicalities. That was Fritz, the former Abwehr general who fought the Nazis from within the system.

Leon was different — a Jew, a writer, what I might call a skeptical dreamer. He came at the Nazi question from the opposite direction. Talking once about the Nazis — having grown up with them in Vienna, long before Hitler was Hitler — Leon said, "They're like fucking cockroaches. You can't kill them all. But you can still have fun poisoning the hell out of most of them."

And I said, "And what about the rest of them?"

"Use them and then abuse them," he said.

Use them and then abuse them. I was repeating that to myself on the boat back to Tallinn, and I guess I wasn't just talking to myself.

"Use who? Abuse who?" Antti said.

"Uh, nobody."

"That must have been some meeting."

"You might say that."

"Want to tell me?"

"Nah," I said.

"I might be able to help. I do have some exper—"

"I don't pay you enough for this kind of shit," I said.

"Well, I didn't say I was going to help you for free."

"And here, I thought we were becoming friends."

"Friends gotta eat, too, bucko," he said.

Then I closed my eyes, and Antti let me be. I drifted in and out of sleep, but I never seemed to let go of the Nazi thread. Helping this Karl Tamm get out of Estonia — I mean, I got it. I heard what Grimm said, and it did make some sense if you viewed the world as a chess board and the West was trying always to stay a few moves ahead of the Commies. I mean, I did understand. I was not an anti-intellectual. I knew how to play chess — if, by playing chess, I meant that I knew how to move the pieces, even if I had to count the squares on my finger before I moved the horse.

But I had changed a lot in the previous decade. To extend the metaphor, I was a lot more prone to turning over the board and letting the pieces fly than I used to be. I had seen too much — in Gestapo jails, in the French Resistance — to remain the passive, don't-make-waves kind of guy who I had been before the war. Somewhere on the boat ride back to Tallinn, I actually had the quickest dream where I was playing chess with Grimm, and decided to fight him, and picked up a piece from the floor after overturning the board, and made a fist, and punched his fucking eye out with the head of the horse that was protruding between my fingers. Thank God that a big swell in the Gulf of Finland woke me up with a crash against the side of the boat, because I really didn't want to know what was going to happen after that.

"Here," Antti said. He handed me a steaming mug of the coffee he made on a small electric ring that he had hooked up to the boat's battery.

"Christ, that's awful," I said.

"You can be a beggar or you can be a chooser."

"Unless I choose to be an ungrateful asshole."

"You said it," he said. "No charge, by the way."

"All part of the service?"

"Because we're becoming friends," he said. Then Antti walked away, back up toward the front of the boat to tend to whatever he tended to on our voyages.

My mind drifted back to Grimm. What he told me about the Forest Brother made the operation seemed doable. This guy, Tamm, lived in the woods outside Tartu. That could work for me. I mean, at least I had been to Tartu. It was where I had driven Linna, and I had met her cousin and his family. That was a place for me to start, anyway. I mean, it wasn't like I needed a map to find it.

The other thing I had was a description of Tamm — and, well, let's just say that if Grimm was even close to accurate, it wasn't going to be hard to pick him out of a crowd. A snapshot would have been better, but the picture in my head would have to do — and it was more than vivid. From what Grimm said,

Tamm was nearly 6 1/2 feet tall, with wild black hair and a black beard — and, also, an oddly long neck.

In Grimm's words: "Imagine if a gorilla fucked a giraffe."

"I'd prefer not to."

"When you see him, you'll understand — or, at least, that's what I've been told."

"It's that striking?"

"The guy who described him to me, after the bit about the gorilla fucking the giraffe, said that Tamm has been known to scare children who see him on his occasional visits to the city. I mean, even if the Soviets hadn't shown up, he'd still probably be living in the forest, just for the sake of the kids."

"Occasional visits?"

"They still need supplies sometimes," Grimm said. "Mostly, they have people who bring them to where they're hiding, but I guess sometimes..."

"You have any names?"

"Names of who?"

"The people who supply him," I said. "The people he might meet with when he does show his face. The places he might go. Family. Friends. Things like that. You know, actual fucking intelligence."

"The description is actual fucking intelligence."

"Which is helpful, yes, but also obtainable from any frightened six-year-old who lives in Tartu. I mean, don't you have an actual organization in place? Isn't that your fucking job, to gather information?"

"My fucking job is to tell you what to do, asshole," Grimm said. "And I've told you."

"And that's all you know?"

"That's more than enough to get started."

"It's cold piss."

"It's more than enough," Grimm said.

That was when, after a long pause, I told him that I would try. And the truth was, the more I thought about it, the more I concluded that my chances of success were at least moderately promising. When Grimm first described the task, I really did think it would be impossible. Now, the more I thought about it, the more I thought that there might be a shot. The odds still weren't in my favor — I mean, the guy looked like a circus freak but still had managed to avoid capture by the Red Army. He clearly had survival skills — oh, and he lived in the goddamned woods. This wasn't going to be easy. I wasn't kidding myself about that.

But I kept coming back to the gorilla fucking the giraffe and the notion that, if nothing else, it was a big advantage that Karl Tamm was likely the ugliest needle in the haystack.

16

I didn't get back to Tartu for more than a week. I needed to think of an excuse for needing the van for a long overnight trip and came up with the notion of going back to visit my fictitious late wife's family.

"I thought they hated you," Linna said.

"And vice versa," I said.

"So, what?"

"There's one brother who wasn't so bad. I've tried to stay in contact, at least a little. And, well, they finally put up the headstone."

I stopped, took a deep breath.

"Well, headstones," I said.

Linna was silent.

"And, well, I guess I just need to see them, just once," I said. "I'm not sure why, but I feel like, I don't know. Have you ever heard of closure? Just the idea of dotting the last i, crossing the last t? Just, I don't know."

"Whatever you need," Linna said, and then she walked away. If we hadn't been in the warehouse, I think she might have hugged me. Then again, it didn't really matter. The conversation had gone just as I had rehearsed it. Dead wife, dead baby, whatever you want, no problem, no questions, no further conversation. It was, as Fritz Ritter had told me, the perfect cover story.

But I went to Tartu instead — not to see Linna's cousin Valter and his wife. They weren't to know about my visit. Instead, I parked in the university district and began looking for their son, Rikkart. The school wasn't that big, and there seemed to be one street where all the bars were, and it was a Thursday night at about 7 p.m. when I got there, and I figured the weekend for the students was likely beginning. But I didn't see him in the first bar I entered, so I tried the next one, The Lantern.

The place was crawling with 20-year-olds. The woman behind the bar was closer to my age. When I leaned in to order, she was in the midst of swatting away the drunken offerings of one of the 20-year-olds.

"You wouldn't be disappointed," he said.

She pointed at his crotch.

"But I heard it's tiny," she said.

"From who?"

"Girls talk."

"I'll show you right now."

"Move along, Tiny," she said, loud enough that two of the kid's buddies heard and began chanting, "Ti-ny, Ti-ny, Ti-ny..."

The kid cursed and walked away, shoving between his chanting friends.

"A job well done," I said.

"It's child's play with these meatheads," she said. "And what brings you here for a visit to my humble menagerie? Don't get many grown-ups at this time of night — and by that I mean, after lunch."

"Looking for a nephew," I said. "Hopefully, one of the more polite meatheads."

"If you say so," she said. Then she handed me a beer and

headed in the direction of a waving kid at the other end of the bar.

As it turned out, Rikkart was sitting in a booth toward the back with four other guys, a pitcher of beer in front of them, a cloud of smoke above them. Rikkart saw me, and it took a second for him to attach my face to my name, and then he stood and hugged me. It was a half-in-the-bag hug, not a full-on-drunk hug. I steered him to a different table, and we began talking about his parents and potatoes and Linna and whatnot.

"So, you fucking her?" Rikkart said.

"Who?"

"Cousin Linna."

"She's my boss."

"So, you can't fuck the boss?"

"Not if you want your dick to remain attached in the morning."

"If you say so," Rikkart said.

At which point, we wandered into a long conversation about sexual droughts, and about the remedies for such. I told him about Leon's theory of the "slump buster," which was how he described a certifiably ugly woman who he slept with to end a dry spell. The way he figured it, "They were grateful, I was grateful, and some of the pressure was lifted."

"But I have standards," Rikkart said.

"Is that what you tell yourself when you're buying a new jar of hand cream?" I said.

At which point, Rikkart burst out laughing and clapped me on the back and went for another pitcher. I watched him walk to the bar and noticed the cloud of smoke along the ceiling, maybe three or four inches thick. I listened and couldn't hear a distinct conversation, but instead, a dozen that melded into a dull roar. The lighting was muted, the bar and the booths were wood, the whole place was dark. It was when he came back that Rikkart finally asked, "So, really, what the fuck are you doing here?"

"It's complicated and it's confidential," I said. "Can I trust you?"

"Of course you can. I mean, you're fucking my cousin. That's almost like family."

"I'm not fucking your cousin."

"Whatever."

"Look, this is serious and maybe a little dangerous," I said. "I'm not kidding around. Can I trust you?"

The word "dangerous" seemed to get Rikkart's attention. The smile disappeared from his face.

"Good," I said. And then I told him that, while I couldn't explain everything, I needed to get a message to one of the Forest Brothers, Karl Tamm.

"Do you ever see them around?"

"I guess," Rikkart said. "Now and again. People steer clear but yeah."

Then Rikkart shouted, "Hey Leks," and waved back toward the booth where he had been sitting. One of the group got to his feet.

"Wait—" I said.

"You can trust him — he's the kid who drew the map for my father. And he'll know."

Leks sat down. I didn't want to trust him but, well, I wasn't sure I had a choice. As it turned out, Leks was more than a cartographer. A lot more. The way the two of them described it, Leks was running a half-dozen shady side businesses, including a small vodka distillery that was headquartered in his dormitory bathtub.

"A man after my own heart," I said.

"A person's got to eat," he said.

We talked some more, and then Rikkart said, "He wants to contact a Forest Brother."

"Doable," Leks said.

"One in particular," I said.

"Go on."

"I've never seen him, but a friend described him as the illegitimate child of a gorilla and giraffe."

Rikkart spat a mouthful of beer. Leks said, "I've seen him. You don't forget."

"Can you get him a message?"

"Probably."

"Not definitely?"

"Depends on where he comes for, shall we say, company," Leks said. He said that, when they needed supplies, the Forest Brothers tended to come for them into town. But when they needed a woman there was an arrangement with a local brothel that the woman would be delivered. He said the madam, one of his vodka clients, explained, "Look, my best clients are Russian soldiers. I can't be having them in one room and one of the Forest Brothers in another. It just, it would just be insulting."

So, the madam had directions into the forest. Most nights, she ran a shuttle service of sorts, delivering girls and vodka. Unless he was wrong, Leks said that he'd be able to arrange for a message to be delivered that night.

"For the right price," he said, and then he went silent. The kid was clearly a skilled negotiator, and he knew that the best negotiating tactic was not the angry demand, but the enduring silence.

I had no time to fool around, so I pulled a roll of bills from my pocket and peeled off enough for Rikkart and Leks to drink in The Lantern for a month, and enough on top of that for every brother in the forest to get his knob polished.

"It has to be tonight," I said.

Leks took the money and said, "Tonight. Absolutely."

"And I need the reply in the morning."

"Where?"

"I'll be staying in town."

Leks looked at the wad of bills and said, "Good. Fine. So, what's the message?"

"It's simple," I said. "One sentence. 'Hansi Brugmann wants you back.'"

The two of them repeated it twice, and then sprinted out the door.

17

I sat at the bar and kept drinking. The bartender — her name was Tuule — pretty much ignored me except to refill my mug. The kids were three deep at the gaps between barstools, trying to get Tuule's attention. Most were Estonian college kids whose verbal skills were deteriorating by the hour. Some, though, were clearly Russians — likely young soldiers on a night off, young soldiers dressed as civilians and proving that there really wasn't much difference between 20-year-old kids, wherever they came from or whatever their level of education. Sex and alcohol really did fuel the world, especially among that age group, and to watch it take place from the remove of my barstool — the chugging, the tentative conversations, the drunken groping — was an anthropological feast.

"This place is a complete circus — what's it like on Friday and Saturday?" I said. Tuule had just refilled my mug for about the fifth time.

"Worse."

"Worse how?"

"Not fucking-in-the-booths worse, but even more crowded and more, well, physical. I have a man work on the weekends, and he just roams around and heads off trouble before it happens. And, well, let's just say that I don't pay him enough."

Then Tuule was off again. I had drunk enough to be a bit unfocused, but I kept returning to the idea of Rikkart and Leks, and about the wisdom of involving them in my scheme to contact Karl Tamm.

The standard rule in these kinds of things was the fewer people involved the better. It just made sense. More people meant more chances for human error. More people, even worse, meant more chances for blabbing, both inadvertent and coerced. I trusted Rikkart because, well, I don't know — it was just a feeling from the first meeting in his parents' living room. How sensible it was to trust my feelings, I didn't know. But it was all I had. And it seemed that if I wanted Rikkart, I had to accept Leks, seeing as how he was the true schemer of the pair.

So, two of them. But what were my alternatives? To sit around Tartu for days on end, hoping to see the progeny of a gorilla and a giraffe stumble out of the woods for provisions? That just wasn't practical. It also was dangerous, at least a little, seeing as how there were Russian soldiers stationed in the city. I didn't need to be explaining my loitering to a cop or to a 22-year-old with a Kalashnikov slung over his shoulder. No, I needed help, and the help I acquired made as much sense as any that might have been possible, and probably more. I mean, I did know Rikkart, and he did have some loyalty to me because of Linna. He and Leks might screw up but they weren't intentionally going to screw me. And, well, what more could I really hope for, given the circumstances?

Besides, all I was asking them to do was deliver a message — or, rather, have a message delivered for them. That was the entirety of it. There was nothing dangerous about it, especially given that it didn't sound as if they would be accompanying the ladies of the night into the night. Get the message delivered, bring me the reply, return to the business of their young, drunk, horny lives. Even if Rikkart and Leks took a ride with them, the girls from the brothel made the same round trip on a daily basis without incident. The risk for them was somewhere between minimal and nonexistent. That's what I kept telling myself when I wasn't having terrible visions of having to tell Linna that something had happened to her cousin's boy.

It was just before 1 a.m. when Tuule flicked the switch on the wall behind the bar, blinking the lights. "Ten minutes," she bellowed, close enough to me that I was startled. She saw me almost flinch my ass off the stool and laughed.

Five minutes later, she blinked the lights again. Five minutes after that, she began physically herding the strays toward the door. When the last one was out, she looked at me and said, "You either help me with the chairs, or you're out, too."

"Chairs it is," I said.

Tuule locked the door and began wiping down tables. I followed behind and picked up the chairs as instructed and turned them upside down over the clean tables. When she was done, Tuule fetched one bucket and two mops.

"Just a lick and a promise," she said. "If it takes more than five minutes for us to finish, we've been too meticulous. I mean, the sticky floor is part of the charm of the place."

We finished in four minutes, and then Tuule headed up a back staircase. I followed her. Her apartment was warm and oddly homey. As it turned out, I was sober enough to perform but drunk enough not to remember much of the before and after conversation, except for the one part when she was making fun of me. I must have been spouting off about my anthropological observations about the sex and alcohol ruling the lives of 20-year-olds, and she said, "You should get a mirror sometime. More lines on your face, and more expensive shoes — but the same rules, it appears to me."

18

I t was light out, and I was half in and out of sleep. I thought I heard someone calling my name in a dream, but it was real life. But I only knew that when Tuule jabbed me in the ribs with her elbow and said, "Someone's yelling for you outside."

I walked over to the open window, navigating through the trail of clothing strewn on the floor — her bra, my underpants, the rest. I stuck my head out the window and it took my eyes a second to focus. It was Rikkart.

"Two minutes," I said. It was more of a croak than anything, but he nodded and leaned against a big trash bin.

I dressed quickly and, I thought, quietly. As I shoved my left foot into my shoe without untying it, Tuule — her eyes closed — mumbled, "Go out the back door, it locks automatically behind you." And, well, so much for sentiment after a night of passion. Though, truth be told, "night of passion" was less accurate than "15 minutes of ravenous lust" — and even that might have been an overstatement of the duration by a factor of, oh, 100 percent. Not that either of us was complaining, though. The last thing Tuule said to me before the poke in the ribs was, "Fast and furious, just like I like it. Fast and furious…" Then she dropped off to sleep.

The back door of the bar did lock behind me, and Rikkart was leaning against the same trash bin when I emerged. He greeted me with a dirty smile and a shake of the head and, "You dirty fucking dog."

"How did you know?"

"Took a shot. You're my fucking hero."

"You're not—"

"Cousin Linna? Who you say you're not fucking? That cousin Linna? I won't tell her. Won't say a word. My lips are sealed. Unlike—"

"Enough," I said.

"Details, man. A morsel. You've got to give me something."

This reminded me of Leon, with whom I had the same kind of conversation every Sunday morning for decades. We would joke later — "Aren't we getting a little too old for details?" — but then, as often as not, we'd spill at least a little. A morsel.

"All right, you fucking child. One morsel. Let's just say that when I took a piss this morning, I noticed a smear of red lipstick when I looked down."

"I knew it," Rikkart said, triumphant.

"All right, before you go home to your hand cream, tell me what happened."

"What?"

"The Forest Brother."

"Oh, right," he said. "The way it worked out, the madam at the bordello didn't want the girls to have the responsibility for delivering the message, so she let us drive them out there."

"How far?"

"Really, not very. The two girls directed us, and it didn't take 15 minutes. We had to go pretty slow — the road, really a path, was pretty narrow and bumpy. But it wasn't that far in. We came to a clearing and gave the signal."

"The signal?"

"Flash the headlights on and off twice, wait a minute, flash them on and off twice again, and then wait. If anyone was interested, they had 10 minutes to get to the clearing. One girl got the back seat, and one took a cot out into the clearing. Five men showed up and they took about, I don't know, 40 minutes."

"And you and Leks?"

"Stood on the other side of the clearing."

"And collected mind pictures for later."

"Between them and you, I'm going to need a new jar of hand cream."

"Your lust aside, was one of the customers—"

"The long-necked freak? Yep. Second man out of the woods. When he got done, the girl told him we wanted a word. He came over, and we told him the message."

"Exactly as I said it."

"Exactly," Rikkart said. "Hansi Brugmann wants you back."

"And?"

"And he said, 'Who sent you?' And I said, 'An agent for Hansi Brugmann.' Was that okay?"

"Sounds good to me. But what did Karl Tamm and his long neck say?"

"He seemed to like it," Rikkart said. "I mean, I said the word 'agent' and he got a little smile on his face. I saw it in the moonlight, just for a quick second."

"And, well?"

"He told us to stay where we were, and disappeared into the woods a few steps. I think he was just taking a piss — I mean, I didn't hear him talk to anybody, and he was back in a minute. Maybe two minutes."

"And?"

"He said, 'Next Friday, 3 o'clock, The Rock.'"

"What's The Rock?" I said.

"A bar at the end of the street where the brothel is. Old man's bar. Total shithole. But it's the closest bar to the entrance into the woods."

"Christ, another week—"

"You didn't tell me to negotiate a time. You just said to bring back the message."

"I'm not mad at you — I'm mad it's going to take another week," I said. "No, you guys did good. But, wait — where's Leks?"

"Well..."

"Let me guess," I said. "Part of his vodka deal with the madam includes—"

"It does indeed."

"He couldn't include you? I mean, if he's really a good mate?"

"He is a good mate. And he did offer. It's just that the deal is with the madam."

"So?"

"With the actual madam," he said. "That's where he is, right now, crawled up with — Christ, she's older than my mother. Like, closer to my grandmother than my mother. Leks says, 'It's all the same in the dark,' but, fuck. I'm hard up, I'll admit that, but hell, nothing's that dark."

I laughed out loud, maybe loud enough for Tuule to hear through the open window, and clapped Rikkart on the back.

"Besides," he said. "I've got some new visions in my head that will carry me for more than a little while."

19

K alma Sauna on Vana-Kalamaja Street was where whoever happened to be working in the warehouse, except for Linna, spent their Wednesday afternoons. It was another perk of the job. There was stuff to do every day, but the big distilling days were Monday and Tuesday and the big delivery days where Thursday and Friday. Wednesday afternoon was a quiet patch for just about everybody. So, Kalma — where we sweated out the beer we were drinking on company time.

We had public saunas growing up in Austria, not that I went very often. They were really saunas and thermal baths, where you would mostly soak in hot water and watch the skin on your fingertips shrivel up. The baths were where the old men would drink the nasty water from a special tap — water that smelled like rotten eggs — and claim that the vile stuff carried some medicinal magic. I never much bought into it, though. It all seemed like something, well, for old men.

In Estonia, though, saunas were like a religion, and I was quickly indoctrinated. The intense heat, the slapping your skin with the birch branches, the cold shower, the cold beer, the rinse, the repeat, and the endless stream of bullshitting that was the persistent undercurrent — I actually came to enjoy it, all of it. More than one of the guys from the warehouse told me of the thrill they felt when their fathers considered them old enough to join their men's sauna group, to be one with the sagging bellies and man-tits on the double-decker wooden benches.

The conversation that Wednesday afternoon was about the Forest Brothers. I had nudged it along at the beginning, doing the dumb foreigner thing, saying that one of my deliveries was talking about them the other day and I was hoping to learn some more.

"I mean, I know the basics," I said.

"You don't know shit," Branko said.

"Did you fucking have to?" Artur said. He was just walking into the sauna, late because he had been stuck for a few minutes in his office with a balance sheet that wasn't balancing.

"What do you mean?"

"You'll see," Artur said.

At just about that point, the yelling began. I mean, it wasn't at the "fuck you/no, fuck you" stage of things, but the heat in the hot box was clearly turned up more than a few degrees. People were talking over each other, but the two phrases that seemed to be repeated the most were "fucking Nazis" and "goddamned patriots" — except when it was "goddamned Nazis" and "fucking patriots."

"Everybody shut the fuck up," I yelled. Surprisingly, they all listened. Then I said, "I really want to understand this. Look, one at a time."

I pointed at Branko.

"One minute, no interruptions, deal?"

I looked around and nobody said anything. Branko was the apparent leader of the "fucking Nazis" camp. He spoke in a low voice, low and sad, about how the Forest Brothers joined up with the Nazis when they took over Estonia and did their dirty work in those couple of years during the war, how they extorted some Jews who were in hiding and exposed the rest.

I mouthed a one-word question as I glanced toward Artur: "Jewish?"

Artur mouthed back, "His wife."

"They worked for fucking animals," Branko said. "They cheered them. They applauded them. They kissed their asses. They tried to imitate them and they took their money. They worked for them, and they fucking enjoyed it."

"Ancient history now," Vladdy said. At which point, all of the shouting and talking over each other began again.

I yelled a second time, and it worked again.

"Your turn, Vladdy," I said, and it was quiet again as he began with the same three words: "Ancient history now."

He told the flip side of the Forest Brothers story, how they were fighting against the Soviets the first time they took over, and how they were forced to hide in the woods when the Soviets retook the country at the end of the war, and how they have formed the backbone of whatever resistance exists against Stalin's rule.

"The first time, I don't care what you say, that was pure patriotism," Vladdy said. "The rest of the country sat on its ass and watched the tanks roll in. Nobody did anything. Nobody but them. And it's the same now. Nobody does anything. Nobody but them."

It was a real hit-and-run resistance, though — Vladdy left that part out. It was the occasional petrol bomb tossed into a vehicle, the odd sniper taking out a couple of Soviet soldiers wandering around and minding their own business. They were a nuisance and little more. And, after a big Soviet operation to clean out the forest just a few months earlier, most people believed that the Forest Brothers numbered in the hundreds at that point, no longer in the thousands or even tens of thousands.

"Those men, those patriots, are the only thing keeping us from—"

"Keeping us from what?" Branko said. "From fucking what? There are Soviet soldiers on the streets. There are Soviet secret police, Christ, they're everywhere. We share a parking lot with their prison, for fuck's sake — and it's not like the cells are empty. The Russians can do whatever they want in this country — can do and are doing. The Forest Brothers, all they're doing is getting hard reminiscing about Hitler and jerking each other off in the woods. They aren't a pimple on Stalin's ass."

At which point, the rules of polite debate were pretty much in the dustbin. I tried to focus in on the "fucking Nazi" side of the shouting, to see if there was any whiff of the stuff Gerhard Grimm had told me about the mass grave and saplings that were planted as camouflage — but there was nothing like that being said. It was all still very much a secret, at least from the general public.

Anyway, within only a few seconds, we did reach the "fuck you/no, fuck you" stage of the proceedings. The only thing that calmed everyone down was the fact that 20 minutes were up, and it was hot as hell in the sauna, and a cool-down and another beer were imperative. When we reassembled, Artur wisely raised a new topic: the ample ass on the sauna owner's teenage daughter. With that, the Forest Brothers debate was forgotten and the last 20 minutes of heat, and then the last beer, were as relaxing and enjoyable as advertised. As religions went, the Estonian sauna had some real potential.

20

He rest had gone ahead, but because Artur arrived late, he stayed for one more round in the sauna. I stayed with him because there were still two more unopened beers. We were dressed and sitting in the lobby of the place, finishing off the beers. The teenage daughter with the big ass had left the front desk to tend to whatever, and we were alone.

"Look, I have something I need to talk to you about," Artur said.

He sounded serious, but I couldn't quite figure what it might be about. I hadn't done anything wrong at work. I didn't fiddle with my collections, not even a little. I turned over every last bit of the cash that I received — every last bit, every time, even if skimming was an accepted part of the job description. "Just a sip of the cream," is how the practice was explained, and nobody seemed to mind. But, the way I figured it, I was being paid by the Gehlen Organization and by Linna, and two salaries were sufficient.

"Okay, shoot," I said.

"This is personal," Artur said. Again, I was left to wonder. We got along fine, the two of us, but it wasn't as if we were close friends.

"Okay," I said, with just the hint of a question mark at the end.

"I know we're not great friends, and that's part of the reason. You not being from here, it helps. You being, I don't know, a little smarter than the rest of those assholes, and maybe a little more mature..."

"A mature asshole, then," I said. "That was a station to which I had always aspired."

"Well—"

"That would look great on the tombstone."

"But seriously—"

"Sorry," I said. And then Artur took a deep breath and just let it all out in one quick burst:

"I'm homosexual and I think an NKVD agent might know."

Christ. Homosexuals had never been on my radar for very long. We laughed about the bar they had in Vienna when we were kids, and the word "homo" was an all-purpose slur among our teenage friends, but it died off as a thing as we grew older. I guess, when you live through two world wars, there are bigger concerns. There were one or two who I fought with in the Paris Resistance, I was pretty sure — but, again, bigger concerns. Since then, I hadn't spent much time thinking about it either way.

So, when Artur said it, I wasn't sure how to react. I went with my standard, a joke. As in, "Well, I'm glad you waited until we got our pants on before telling me."

Artur smiled, and then went quiet, and then said, "I knew I could trust you."

"What do you mean?"

"The joke. That told me all I needed to know that I could

trust you." He thought for a second and then said, "Mature asshole. Exactly right."

I didn't know what to say, and given that Artur had told me the difficult part, I didn't know what he was waiting for. But it took him another few seconds before the rest came tumbling out.

"You know the Bastion Passages, right?"

"Heard of them. Air raid shelters, right?"

"During the Soviet bombing, yes," he said. "But before that, just a way for soldiers in the old days to get from place to place within the fortress..."

"At the Kiek in de Kok?"

"Yes."

"Interesting name to be introduced into this conversation, if you understand any dirty English slang."

Artur shrugged. We were talking in English, as we usually did, but neither of us was anything close to being native speakers. He knew that in German, "kiek in de Kok" roughly meant "peek into the kitchen," which is what you could do from the high tower windows — look down, peek into the windows of the houses below, shoot at infidels from a hell of a vantage point. When I went to the gutter English, with an emphasis on the "Kok," he laughed and shook his head and said again, "Mature asshole."

Then he said, "The tunnels are pretty much abandoned now. And they are a place where, well, where men of similar interests can sometimes have a quiet meeting. And, well, I was leaving the tunnels one night with someone, and we were confronted by Krutov."

"Krutov?"

"Never met him?" Artur said. "He's NKVD. His office is in the prison, right across the parking lot. I don't deal with those people, but I have seen him. Linna does the talking, but I have been in the same room with him once or twice — months ago, but still."

"So what happened?"

"He stopped us, made a few leering suggestions, but let us go."

"So, what's the problem?"

"I could see that he recognized me," Artur said. "I mean, I'm pretty sure — you can just tell sometimes, right? And he made a remark about how we better not have left a vodka bottle behind, or he would get us for littering."

"That's not much—"

"I'm telling you, it was the whole vibe. And at the end, he looked at me — not at my friend — and said, 'I'm sure I'll be seeing you again, Artur.' He knew my name, and I hadn't told him. I had never told him. I had never been introduced to him. I had never said a word to him in those couple of meetings. I stood in the back of the room and said nothing. Like, literally nothing. How did he know my name?"

So, it wasn't the product of an overactive imagination after all. Krutov knew his name. That pretty much settled it. Artur was almost out of breath after he got that last bit out. He stopped for a second to calm himself.

"Look, he could throw me in jail tomorrow. He could get me fired from the only job I've ever actually been good at. Or, he could—"

"Blackmail you."

"Exactly," Artur said. "That's the one I probably fear the most. I mean, I just don't think that I could live that way."

He stopped. I thought.

"So, what do you think I can do about it?" I said.

He said nothing.

"I mean, who do you think..."

He said nothing, not for a minute. Maybe more. The silence

was beyond uncomfortable. Artur seemed to start talking and then stopped — once, then a second time.

Finally, he said, "Look, I don't know your story. I mean, I know the story you tell, but I think it's bullshit. No offense, but I think it's bullshit."

I started to interrupt him, but he put up his hand and plowed ahead.

"Your life, your business. And I've told you something about me, but only because I'm desperate and because I need help. I don't expect the same in return. I don't expect anything, I guess. But it just seems to me that you've got way too much on the ball to be driving a fucking delivery truck. You're too smart to get stuck in this fucking place."

"You seem to be forgetting that the back half of 'mature asshole' is 'asshole,' and that sometimes, bad things happen to—"

He held up his hand again, and I stopped talking. I wasn't going to admit anything about my true purposes, and Artur seemed smart enough to realize that. At the same time, he knew — and if that was disconcerting on the one hand, it wasn't all that surprising that a reasonably intelligent person who interacted with me on a regular basis could guess that I was playing some kind of angle. That meant Artur might know, and Linna might know, and that was pretty much it. The rest were honestly too stupid to figure it out or too self-absorbed to care.

But, well, what could I do to help? I had no idea.

"Krutov hasn't contacted you yet?" I said.

"No, nothing."

"And how long has it been?"

"Four days."

"Might blow over."

"You really think so?" he said.

"No," I said.

I asked him a couple of more questions — about where he lived, his family, things like that — but I was just stalling for time. I asked him how none of our co-workers or Linna had figured out his secret and he laughed and said, "Strategic hetero-sexuality."

"Meaning?"

"The occasional comment, like when I brought up the daughter with the big ass back there," he said. "And, maybe once a year, I get loaded enough and leave the bar after work with someone. A female someone."

The question I had not asked must have been evident on my face, because Artur smiled and said, "The equipment seems to work either way."

Then it was my turn to go quiet for an uncomfortable period of time — not because of Artur's equipment, but because of the whole rest of it. This really was outside of my remit. Fritz Ritter and the Gehlen people would be furious if they ever found out, not that it had ever stopped me before.

Still, this was different. I was a long way from home, and the NKVD wasn't exactly a scout troop. That any involvement on my part could end up catastrophically went without saying.

Finally, I said, "Let me look into it."

Artur smiled. The owner's daughter with the fat ass was back behind the front desk, and we handed her the empties.

"No promises," I said.

Artur held the door for me and he was still smiling.

21

I t was a couple of days later when Artur and I hit the NKVD daily double. First was the message waiting for him on his desk when he arrived at the warehouse. His hands were shaking when he handed it to me.

Artur,

Enjoyed our chat the other night at the passages. We need to catch up further. I'll be in touch, likely soon.

Krutov

"Not very subtle," I said.

"I'm going to fucking puke on the desk," Artur said.

"Calm down."

He leaned over and unloaded into a small metal trash can next to the desk. Just then, Branko walked by and poked his head in the office door and said, "Fucking vodka will kill you." The truth was, very few days went by when one of the employees didn't throw up in a trash can or a sink or the alley behind the building.

I shut the office door. Artur retched twice more then wiped his mouth on a rag that he pulled from the desk drawer.

"Well, what do you think?" he said.

"I think our fears have been realized."

"Christ. Fuck."

"Yeah, pretty much," I said.

"Have you—"

"Thought of anything? Not exactly. It's kind of, well, I don't know what I don't know. I need to find out more about Krutov, and researching the background of an NKVD agent isn't exactly a cinch. I mean, it isn't as if his information is all in a telephone directory."

"But," Artur said, and then he stopped himself and thought. Then he said, "But maybe if you just waited for him to leave work, and maybe got to him in a quiet place, you could—"

"I'm not a fucking assassin, Artur. Look, I don't know what you really think of me, deep down, but I'm not a fucking assassin. I'm not a gun for hire. Get that out of your head right now."

"If not that, then—"

"You're going to have to trust me there," I said. "Look, the timetable is obviously accelerated now. I want you to tell Linna that I'm taking a few days off for a personal reason. She'll be okay with it."

"I don't know," he said. "Just based on her body language lately, I get the sense she thinks something squirrelly is already going on with you."

"Not your concern."

"Are you fucking her?"

"Why does everybody think that?"

"I don't think everybody does," he said. "Just a shot in the dark. Don't worry about it. I can keep a goddamned secret."

"Look, just tell her," I said. "I'll get my deliveries done early — I'll finish by tonight. I'm probably going to need a week or so. You're going to have to schedule my replacement — just have it done before you tell her, and that will give her less of a chance to object. But she won't."

"If you say so."

"I'm also going to need a vehicle," I said.

Artur opened the same desk drawer that held his barf rag and pulled out a set of keys.

"Black Saab," he said. "Or, to be perfectly accurate, ancient black Saab. But it runs fine. It's out back, on the next block."

"Yours?"

"Well, sort of. I accepted it in trade once from a bar owner out in the sticks. I fiddled with the books, and Linna never caught on. If she ever did, well, that's why I keep it parked on the next street over, when I'm not using it. I'd just tell her I felt sorry for the guy, and that I hadn't gotten around to selling it, but that we'd be whole when I did. It looks like fried shit but, like I said, it runs fine and the tank's full."

I took the keys, loaded up the panel truck until the springs sagged as low as grandpa's ass, and made my deliveries. Two of the stops didn't have the cash because I was a day or two early, and I told them they could slide until the next week. We did it all the time for our regulars. Friendly bootleggers, we were.

It was after dark when I pulled into the warehouse parking lot. Everybody was gone for the night. I went inside and hung the keys on the appropriate hook and dropped the collections I was able to make on Artur's desk blotter. It was when I was walking out of the back door, fingering the Saab keys in my pocket, when I saw the two men in black trench coats get out of the black sedan parked near the gate.

"Alex Kovacs?" said the guy on the left.

"Yes."

"Come with us, please," said the guy on the right.

That they were NKVD/MVD/Whatever-the-hell went without saying. Why they drove across the parking lot from the prison didn't make much sense, though. When I started walking toward the prison gate, the first one said, "No, in the car."

"But, aren't you—"

The second one laughed and said, "No, we're not them. Those animals are in fucking Siberia. We have a proper office. Get in the car."

My initial thought had been that this had something to do with Artur. The fact that we were heading downtown, well, that changed the calculus. To what, I wasn't sure. But it wasn't as if I didn't have a new set of worries.

We were at the headquarters building inside of 10 minutes, and it would have been quicker if they had used the siren. They parked in front, not in the alley alongside. They took me in the main door, past the front desk, and up the stairs. The three of us walked to nearly the end of the hallway, several offices past the one where I had photographed the duty rosters that were hanging on the clipboards. The door was open, and I was left with another black suit who identified himself as Captain Igor Kuznetzov. He sat in his chair and pointed me to one of the two wing chairs across from his desk.

After a bit of conversational fumbling, we settled on Estonian. His was slightly better than mine, it seemed, but only slightly. It would be a fair verbal fight, but I was under no illusions that any of the rest of it would be equitable.

After a few basic questions, and my producing the fabulously phony Estonian citizenship papers that Fritz Ritter had supplied before I left Vienna, Kuznetzov handed the document back, opened the middle desk drawer, and removed a photograph blown up to 8 x 10 size. He pushed it across the blotter, and I leaned over and picked it up.

It was a picture of me.

I wasn't a virgin in these kinds of situations, and I knew how important it was for my face to betray nothing, not in any situation, not after any provocation. I studied the photo for maybe three seconds, and knew immediately that it was blurry enough that there was no way for anyone to use it for a beyond-any-reasonable-doubt kind of identification. The truth was, I knew for sure that it was me only because of the watch cap and the eyeglasses I had worn that night.

One second. Two seconds. Three. Then I leaned over and half flipped/half placed it back on the desk blotter. I did that and I said, "So, who is he?"

I made sure to make eye contact, and I maintained it until Kuznetzov looked down to put the photograph back into the desk drawer.

"New technology," he said. "The camera is mounted to the wall in the lobby. After hours, any time the door opens, a photograph is taken every 10 seconds for the next 30 seconds. A great Soviet advance."

I nodded my assent and tried not to show how quickly my mind was racing. Where were the glasses and the watch cap? In the delivery truck? No, in my apartment — but not hidden beyond sharing a drawer with my socks and underpants. Even a lame-ass search would uncover them in about two minutes.

Did they already have them? Hard to know. But my play was obvious — to act as if they knew nothing. To play dumb. It was all I had.

"A little while back, a white panel truck like the one you often drive was seen parked in the alley next to this building," Kuznetzov said.

"Wasn't me — I've never been here," I said. I debated in my head about how scared I should try to make myself appear to be. On the one hand, I didn't want to appear weak. On the other hand, a civilian sitting in my seat would likely be leaving wet spots on the upholstery. So I tried for a middle ground.

"I mean, uh, I guess I've driven past here before," I said, and I tried to make my voice shake just a little. "But there have to be lots of white panel trucks in Tallinn. I mean, hundreds. Black sedans and white panel trucks."

"Yes, I'm aware," Kuznetzov said. "Two soldiers died that night."

"Oh, that's terrible. But, I mean, I've never—"

Kuznetzov put up his hand and I stopped talking.

"There was evidence of vodka on the scene of their murders. You deliver vodka for a living."

I said nothing.

"Illegally."

I said nothing.

"Under the protection of my comrades at Patarei Prison."

Again, nothing.

"Vodka, white panel truck, and the photograph," Kuznetzov said. "Could be you. A little blurry, but could be you."

"But, but, captain—"

Again, Kuznetzov put his hand up. Again, I stopped talking and prayed that whatever emotion was showing on my face was believable. Inside, the details of the night kept whirling through my consciousness: the broken bottle I picked up, the spilled vodka that I pissed over, the money I stole from the wallets, the soldiers' pants that I pulled down, the quiet thuds of the silenced pistol shots. The quiet thuds, most of all.

The truth was, the photograph wasn't enough to identify me. The truth was, there were hundreds of white panel trucks in Tallinn, maybe thousands. The truth was, whatever vodka had spilled on the bodies or been found in their systems was not traceable to me or the warehouse. The truth was, every desk in the building — Kuznetzov's included — probably had a bottle stashed in the bottom drawer, so believing that two soldiers were drinking on duty was hardly a stretch.

Even though I killed those two pathetic bastards, the truth was that they couldn't come close to proving it. Then again, proof was a relative term when you were dealing with the NKVD/MVD/Whatever-the-hell.

I waited. I made more eye contact, pleading eye contact. This time, Kuznetsov didn't let go, not for a good 10 seconds, not until he said, "That's all for now, Mr. Alex Kovacs. We'll contact you if we have any more questions."

I walked out the front door and made a point of not only keeping my head down but blowing my nose as I walked, making doubly sure that the camera wouldn't catch my face if it was turned on. I walked a full block before dropping to my knees and throwing up in the gutter.

22

The Rock was, indeed, the shithole that Rikkart had described. The only thing more disgusting than the decor was the clientele. There were three men sitting at the bar, old men. One was face down, the other two more catatonic than anything — and they all smelled as if they had not bathed in a month. The only redeeming feature of the place was one of those booths in the back that was actually a bit of a private nook, with a half-height set of swinging doors at the entrance.

"OK for me?" I said to the bartender, pointing at the nook. I had ordered three beers, and he was drawing them.

"Suit yourself. Just, no sleeping allowed."

"Or sex, presumably."

"You look more like a sleeper," the guy said, and then he pushed the three mugs in my direction.

Rikkart was with me. I handed him one of the beers and pointed to a table outside the nook.

"Point him in here when he arrives, but nobody but the giraffe," I said.

"And if there's more than him? And if they disagree with your seating arrangements?"

"Just make some noise, and I'll come out."

As it turned out, Karl Tamm was about 10 minutes late, and he was alone. I tried not to stare as he sat himself down and then took a long pull from the mug, but it didn't take more than a glance to see that this was one freakish human — unruly black hair, never-trimmed black beard, and that neck. Giraffe-ish really was the only suitable description.

Tamm finished the beer in two and I shove mine across.

"Here, I haven't touched it," I said.

"Either way," he said. That one, too, was gone in two big gulps.

"So, what am I doing here?" he said. "I mean, who the fuck are you?"

"Just the messenger," I said. In my head, the way I said it was, "Just the messenger, asshole," but I kept the last part to myself. Instead, I stood up and talked over the swinging doors to Rikkart, telling him to get us two more beers. I stood and waited until he brought them, and watched as Tamm downed another one in two. I sipped on mine and kept my hand locked around the mug.

"So, how do you know Hansi?" he said.

"I don't."

"Then, what the fuck—"

"Easy, big guy," I said, and immediately regretted it. Then again, what the hell? "Big guy" was likely the nicest description anyone had ever attached to him. I mean, it wasn't as if I called him a long-necked freak.

Still, I couldn't let him react, just in case.

"Like I said, I'm only the messenger. Hansi Brugmann has been in contact with the guy I talk to, and I was told to find you and deliver the message."

"And that's it?"

"All I fucking got."

"And I'm supposed to just pick up and follow your skinny ass back to who-knows-where? I mean, who the fuck do you think I am?"

"I don't know who you are," I said. "I don't know, and I don't particularly care. Look, if you just want to go back to shitting in the woods and fucking whores in the woods, knock yourself out. I'm just delivering a message — and, if you agree, I deliver you to my friend, who delivers you to this Hansi Brugmann, who is apparently somebody who you know from I-don't-know-where. But I get paid either way once the message is delivered."

I sipped the beer, put it down, and folded my arms in front of me — the universal body language for, "Well, what'll it be, asshole?" Tamm reached over and grabbed my beer and downed the rest in one, and then belched loud enough to wake the guy sleeping on the bar.

While I waited, Rikkart appeared over the half-height swinging doors, holding two more beers. I walked over while Tamm stewed.

"I figured," Rikkart said.

"Good lad."

This time, Tamm sipped and I sipped. I couldn't begin to understand the calculation that he might be making as he sat there, and I figured there was no sense interrupting him with questions or fake assurances. And even though the guy was scary as shit — and no doubt had a weapon of some sort in his jacket pocket, probably a knife — I didn't feel overly scared.

My biggest concern was that I would have said my piece and he would have jumped over the table and pummeled the life out of me, all the while screaming, "Hansi Brugmann is dead, motherfucker." The odds there were so slim, though. It wasn't as if they broadcast news of former minor Nazi officers dying in

German prisons on an hourly basis. I mean, honestly — "Nazi officer dies in prison" was significantly less newsworthy in Germany than "Clouds expected tomorrow."

And even if it had been on the radio, hell — what were the odds that the Forest Brothers had a shortwave set tuned to whatever local broadcast might have contained the news? They probably didn't have battery power for an hour a day to spend on civilian news broadcasts, given the need to monitor local Soviet army movements. They probably didn't have an hour a week.

No, Tamm didn't know the truth about Brugmann. Hell, he would have jumped Rikkart first, back in the forest clearing, if he already knew. No, it was clear that this freak was intrigued — intrigued but uncertain.

Three sips in, he said, "So, how would it work?"

"How would what work?"

"If I came with you?"

"I have a vehicle here in Tartu. I would drive you back to Tallinn and hide you out for as long as it took me to arrange a boat to Helsinki."

"How long?" he said.

"Probably hours, maybe a day."

"And, then?"

"I take you to my contact in Helsinki, and he takes you to Brugmann."

More silence, more sips.

"But... why?" Tamm said.

This is the question I had been anticipating, and I had practiced the answer for days. Why?

"Look," I said, and then I leaned forward and lowered my voice just a little. I was hoping for a conspiratorial tone, and I was pretty sure, by the look on Tamm's face, that he was drawn in.

"You can tell, I think, that I'm German," I said.

"I thought so!" Tamm said.

"I know I said before that I'm only the messenger, but I do know a little bit more. I know Brugmann was your commanding officer when he was here. I know you worked together, and that your group was especially tight-knit. Right so far?"

Tamm sipped, then nodded.

I fumbled a few times with my words — I had practiced the fumbling, too — and then I said, "Look, Brugmann is part of a group that, let's just say, believes that the Nazi Party has some unfinished business in this part of the world. He and they are trying to, shall we say, reassemble some of the best men remaining in order to, how can I put this...?"

"Restore some fucking order," Tamm said.

"Exactly — well put."

"And he wants me?"

"It's more like 'needs' than 'wants,' I think — but, then again, I'm just reading body language and tone of voice, what I got from my contact. But, yes, he certainly wants you. I mean, this is an incredible pain in the ass for me, coming way out here — a pain in the ass, and risky, and dangerous — and it jeopardizes other work I'm doing."

"Other work?" Tamm said, suddenly eager.

"I've said too much already. But that's where it is."

I folded my arms again. He finished his beer and then the rest of mine. I had made my best pitch, and it was a good pitch. But all Tamm did was stare down at the empty mug for another minute, stare and talk to himself silently, his lips actually moving a couple of times.

Then, suddenly, as if struck by a brainstorm, he stood up and said, "Same time, same place, next week."

Before I could say anything, he was through the swinging doors and out into the bar. About three seconds later, I heard the front door of the place swing open on unoiled hinges and then slam shut. Only then, with Rikkart looking at me over the half-doors, did I look at the ceiling and yell, "Fuck."

23

Trips like this, Antti called them, "Just a jaunt on the great circle route." What he meant was, we would leave Tallinn and, instead of going all the way to Helsinki, just travel in an arc for an hour in the Gulf of Finland before returning to where we started. About halfway out was when I would send the radio message to Gerhard Grimm.

It was a pain in the ass to do it that way, but Grimm was right — the risk in Tallinn was too big. Radio detection equipment was getting better all the time, just as my little sending radio was getting better, too. But it had always been dangerous, always and forever. I never picked up the damn sending key without thinking of Gregory, who I allowed to help me with the radio in Zurich in 1939, and who ended up dead because of it. Gregory got killed and his son Henry — one of my best friends — killed our friendship right then, too. Alex, Leon and Henry. My Uncle Otto used to call us the Three Musketeers, but Gregory always called us the Three Degenerates. They were both right. God, I missed those times.

The radio fit in my coat pocket, about the size and weight of a brick cut in half. I was able to hook it up to the boat's battery,

and that's how I sent the message. We had a standing agreement
— any message from me had to be sent between 10 and 11 p.m.
He guaranteed that he would be listening at that time on
Mondays, Wednesdays, and Fridays — and the truth was, both
of the previous times I had sent anything, his reply arrived
within minutes. We didn't use a code, just some random disguise
words if that was required. If the message was as simple as
asking for a meeting, there was no need to obfuscate. I would
ask for the meeting and he would reply with the time. The place
was always Suomenlinna. He was never dragging his ass over to
me in Tallinn.

But this was different, so I had to be specific without being
too specific. Really, it wasn't hard.

We were out for about 45 minutes when I hooked up the
cable to the battery, and then tuned to the frequency by
moonlight.

"Need anything?" Antti said.

"Nah, all good."

"Can't be that good if you need to check in with the asshole."

"Now that you mention it," I said. And then, for a reason I
still can't understand, I told him the whole story — my mission
to contact the progeny of a gorilla and a giraffe named Karl
Tamm, to get him back from the forest by pretending he was
being summoned by his former Nazi commander.

"But the Nazi's really dead, right?" Antti said.

"Right."

"So, why do they want the giraffe guy?"

"I'm not sure..."

I stopped myself, but just for a second.

"Fuck it," I said, and then I explained to him about the Jews
they executed, and the mass grave, and the saplings they planted
on top, and the need to keep that secret from the Soviets, and
the reality that Tamm was likely the last person who knew it.

"Shit," was all Antti said. He walked away and poured two cups of his terrible coffee and then handed me one.

"It goes without saying that all of this has to stay between us, and especially the fucking last part," I said.

"No kidding."

"I'm serious."

"So am I, bucko — serious as a heart attack. I know all about keeping secrets. Some of the shit I know, it would curl your hair."

We both drank our coffee, and then I began to fiddle with the radio frequency again, and then Antti asked, "So, why this?"

"Because Tamm is jerking me around."

"Won't come for his old beloved Nazi commander?"

"He seems intrigued, but he's delaying — and I have other shit to do, and to tell you the truth, this Tamm thing scares me a little. I don't know why — maybe it's just because the guy is a fucking fright to sit across a table from. But, like, I don't know who the hell I trust."

"You seem to trust me."

"I'm not sure about that, either."

"Fuck you, too. But really, I'll help you but I have no idea how."

"Thanks, old man," I said. "I don't know, either. Just let me send this fucking message, and then we can get off the water and thaw our asses out."

The message, as it turned out, was easy enough. I checked my watch: 10.12 p.m.

It didn't take two minutes to send:

"Our brother has cold feet. Don't feel like begging any longer. Advise."

I plugged the little earpiece into the side of the radio and cupped my other ear with my hand. Antti watched me and seemed to know that I couldn't talk while trying to listen for the reply.

It came within five minutes. Grimm the asshole was nothing if not prompt. I jotted down the dots and dashes on a little notepad and then translated them. There must have been some garble, though, and I couldn't quite figure out what I had. So I sent another message, one word: "Repeat." It didn't take long, and this one seemed a little briefer.

"What did he say?" Antti asked when I got done writing.

"He said, and I quote, 'Try harder. Imperative. Repeat imperative.'"

I tore the sheet off of the pad and tossed it into the gulf. I mean, I didn't expect anything different, but I guess I hoped for maybe a little sympathy, or maybe a little suggestion about tactics. I didn't even want to think about what I would do if Tamm went from intrigued to hostile in the space of the coming week.

24

S t. Nicholas Orthodox Church was on Vene Street in the old part of Tallinn, a couple of blocks away from the post office where Linna's father was killed in the Soviet bombing. It wasn't big and sprawling, but, well, tidy — pale stone, a bell tower, a couple of other turret-y elements, interesting enough. And, well, whatever.

The service was scheduled to start at 10 a.m., and I was taking a flyer that Krutov would be in attendance. The reason was simple enough: his home was only a few blocks away. After Artur had hidden behind a battlement on the warehouse roof and pointed him out to me, I had managed to tail Krutov home out of the parking lot without any trouble. On the one hand, it seemed odd to me that he didn't appear to be paying much attention to who might or might not be following him. Then again, maybe it wasn't odd at all. He was the hunter, not the hunted. That was his identity, his truth. He and the rest of the NKVD, they were the big swinging dicks in Tallinn. What did they have to worry about?

Still, following him home was the sum total of the progress I had made on figuring out a plan to save Artur. Even then, I wasn't sure about the exact house, only the one where Krutov had parked in front. Hell, I still didn't even know his first name.

I was in place, across the street from the church, at 9.45. I chose a spot that, if Krutov walked in the way I expected, he would be unlikely to spot me. It was a sunny day, and I was sitting on a garden wall in front of a middling-sized stone house, my head tilted back. I was, by all appearances, catching some restorative rays on my face — nothing more, nothing less — but I could still see the entrance of the church through the slits of my eyes. It would do.

At 9.55, I saw them, four of them, Krutov and what undoubtedly were his wife and his two daughters. They looked to be pretty close in age — say, 12 to 14 years old. The quick math put them as pre-war babies, before Hitler and Stalin interrupted the cozy family life of a torturer-in-training. As I watched them walk — him in a brown suit, not the NKVD-standard black everything, his wife and daughters in smart-looking dresses — I could only guess at Krutov's career path. I mean, the cream of the cream were not being shipped out to Tallinn. I had to think that the really accomplished knuckle-breakers got the plum jobs in Moscow, and then it went geographically from there. And while I guessed that a posting to Tallinn was better than one to the ass-end of Siberia, I wasn't sure.

Right near the church entrance, I couldn't make out what he said from across the street, but Krutov did say something to his wife and daughters, and they did all start laughing, and the wife did give him a punch on the shoulder and a very loud, "Oh, Konstantine!" So, I had a full name now, Konstantine Krutov, and the outlines of his personal life.

That was something, without doubt, but I wasn't sure where it got me. Still, something was something, and I accepted my victory and moved on. I had no idea what my next step might be, other than to follow him some more. I thought about a midafternoon watch outside of his house, maybe from the end of the street, in case he was a Sunday-drink-with-the-fellas kind of villain. Then again, if he was an afternoon-nap kind of villain, I'd be wasting hours for nothing. I debated it for a while and then decided that, either way, I would have a couple of hours to kill. Besides, I would need to change my jacket and put on the watch cap and glasses, just as a bit of standard tradecraft.

My sleeping patterns were so irregular — just a feature of the job — and I wasn't getting any younger, and I always seemed tired. My intention was to take a nap of my own, but when I reached my apartment, I found Linna sitting on the front steps.

"Don't tell me you were at church?" she said.

"Okay, I won't tell you."

About two minutes later, we were naked on the kitchen floor, of all places, and I was beginning my customary explorations. When I paused for a breath, she grabbed the back of my head and said, "Don't let God stop you."

"No worries, heaven can wait," I said.

25

L inna chose the restaurant for lunch. It was away from the older part of Tallinn, in the general direction of the warehouse but not even halfway there. It was closer to the Kalma Sauna than anything, maybe four blocks away. It was called Dmitri's, and the food was the standard Estonian shit, pork and potatoes in every conceivable form, covered in some kind of brown sauce. As I sawed through it, I tried to remember the last time I'd had a decent schnitzel. Probably close to six months. It was with Leon, back in Vienna. He was bitching about how bad the newspaper had become, and I was asking him why he didn't just quit, and he speared a piece of meat from the plate and said, "Because veal doesn't grow on trees, asshole. We're not all independently wealthy like you."

I didn't like to think about it, but if I wasn't independently wealthy, I was within shouting distance. I had saved by living a frugal life while simultaneously taking every advantage of my expense account as a traveling sales rep before the war. Then I had a big inheritance from my uncle, and I made real money besides during my pre-war stint in Czech intelligence, posing as a bank president in Zurich. The truth was, I didn't need my salary from the Gehlen Organization. The truth was, shouting distance was really whispering distance.

Anyway, the food was shit, and Linna and I had little to say to each other. Well, except for when she asked me, "So, how's your thing going, back in the sticks?"

"Don't ask," I said.

"I am interested, you know."

"And I am very conscious of the boundaries you set up at the beginning of this, this, this whatever you call it between us. And, well, it's just hard to talk about. I hope you can understand."

And that was pretty much it. She still thought I was somehow wrestling with the death of my wife and our infant child, going back to see the graves and reconnect with her family, however tentatively. How much longer I could pull it off, I didn't know. I was going to have to go back to Tartu at least once more to meet with Karl Tamm. I was pretty sure I could sell that one, but after that, well, I wasn't positive. I mean, yes, I was sleeping with her, but Linna was still my boss and the business seemed to come first in her life. It seemed to be her whole life, other than the occasional interlude on my kitchen floor. Then again, I really didn't know anything about her, other than the warehouse and the kitchen floor. For all I knew, she was on a different kitchen floor every day of the week.

After lunch, Linna said she wanted to show me the house where she grew up. It was less than a five-minute walk from the restaurant. It was a skinny wooden structure in the middle of a block full of skinny wooden structures. They looked flimsy, but seeing how old they looked, that was a false impression. The storms off of the gulf were frequent enough that they had taken a battering over the years and were still standing. They just looked like hell.

"Remember how I told you that my father left us on the day of the bombing?" Linna said.

I nodded.

"Well, this was the place. I still remember standing on the porch with my mother and watching him go, and then the two of us with the candles and the tinned food in the cellar, and the booms, and the dust shaking out of the walls."

She sat on the second step leading up to the porch. I sat next to her.

"The fucking Soviet bombs, they hit Telegraaf House and killed my father," she said. "This was later that day. Same day."

She stopped. Her breath caught.

"Same goddamned day," Linna said. "The bombs stopped, and we went outside. The whole block did. We weren't hit, not nearly, but we could see fires. We had no idea about my father. And, well, the Germans were starting to make a run for it. The bombs, they were doing what they were supposed to do — chase the fucking Nazis out of here."

She stopped. Another hiccup of breath.

"But," she said. "But it was still another day before most of them started being evacuated to wherever. Another day, after the bombs fell, when the Nazis just roamed the streets looking... looking..."

Linna stopped another time and sobbed. Again, I never knew what to do with her, but I did put my arm around her, and her face did fall into my chest — but just for a second.

"The fucking Nazi, he was a sergeant," she said. "There was another one with him, and he took me in the other room. The sergeant looked at him and said, 'Lucky Pierre,' but he seemed more afraid than I was. We just sat there while the sergeant dragged my mother upstairs. I remember the screaming, but I mostly remembered the silence after the screaming, if that makes any sense. After a few minutes, there were heavy steps on the staircase, and then the sergeant yelling, 'Did you get yours yet, Lucky Pierre?' He put his fingers to his lips to tell me to stay quiet. Then he left me, and they left the house."

With that, Linna's face fell again into my chest — but, again, only for the briefest instant. Then she was on her feet.

"Come on," she said. "Let's go see Momma."

Inside, the house was tidy enough. In a chair in the corner was a woman who looked 80 but who, Linna said, was only 60. Linna leaned over and said hello and kissed her mother on the forehead, but there was no reply. Actually, there was no response of any kind. Linna's mother was catatonic.

"How long?" I said.

"Since that day."

"Do you live—"

"No, a neighbor helps," Linna said. "I pay her. She bathes Momma, and changes her clothes, and shares her meals. She's compliant enough — tell her it's time for the toilet, and she gets up and walks to the toilet, no problem. Hand her a sandwich, and she eats. But you never get a verbal response. Sometimes, I think I can sense a little bit of recognition in her eyes, that she knows who I am. Most days, though, are like this."

Linna kissed her mother on the head again, and received nothing in reply again, and then we walked over to the warehouse in silence. It was Sunday, and I had nothing to do, and I'm not sure what Linna had to do, but I didn't feel as if I should leave her to walk alone. I left her later, though, still in her office, doing whatever. I left her, and took a bottle of vodka with me, and finished more than half of it in my apartment. That night, when I closed my eyes, all I could see was her mother in that chair in the corner, staring at nothing.

The woman was a shell of a human being, just hollow. Looking at her, both in person and in my mind's eye, I could see a little bit of a resemblance with Linna, but that wasn't what I took out of that visit. March 9, 1944 — that's what I took out of it. March 9, 1944 — the day when the Soviet bombs fell was the day that Linna effectively became an orphan. March 9, 1944 — the day when Linna also become a little bit of a shell of a human being, a little bit hollow.

26

I t was the next morning — I was on time and with a hangover that was manageable, somehow — when Vladdy walked over and handed me an envelope. The reason he handed it to me was that my name was written on the outside.

"It was taped to the door when I opened up this morning," Vladdy said. He was one of the bottling guys, and liked to get here early because the water pressure for cleaning the returns was better before people arrived. It didn't make a lot of sense to me — it wasn't as if people were flushing the toilet constantly, or washing the trucks on more than a weekly basis — but, whatever. Vladdy tended to be the first guy at the warehouse.

"What time—"

"I got here at 6," he said.

It seemed odd. I stuffed the envelope into my jacket pocket and went in to see Artur. When I arrived at his office door, he looked up at me with hopeful puppy dog eyes.

"Anything?"

"A little," I said. I explained that I knew Krutov had a family, and that I knew he had a first name.

"And that helps—"

"How?" I said. "Not sure. But I'm accepting it as progress."

"But—"

"Look, it's a process. I've got some other thoughts about my next move. This is okay. He hasn't sent you another note, has he?"

"Nope."

"Good, then," I said. "There's no reason to get your shit in an uproar until that happens. In the meantime, all I can tell you is that I'm working on it every day. And that's going to have to do for now. Okay?"

Artur nodded and thanked me. I fingered the envelope in my jacket pocket as I headed into the toilets. The last stall had a door that actually locked, and the cleaners were in over the weekend so things weren't nearly as disgusting as they would be by midweek.

I gasped, just a little, when I read the note:

Kiek in de Kok.

Monday, 11 p.m.

It was signed with the letter O, and three lines were drawn beneath it. That was the part that made me gasp because that was how my Uncle Otto used to sign his informal correspondence. Birthday cards, inter-office memos, and little notes of congratulations were signed that way, quickly but distinctively, with the O and three lines. Back when, before the war, it was how I knew for sure that the Gestapo had killed him — because of the O with the three lines beneath it that had been part of the graffiti in one of the cells in the basement of Gestapo headquarters in Cologne.

It meant one thing, of course. It meant that Fritz Ritter was in Tallinn to see me. It was the one true way he could signal that it was him without saying his name. It was the one way, because he had been Otto's running buddy way back, two single men who occasionally ran into each other on the road and did what single men on the road tended to do.

They met in Munich in the 1920s, just two guys on neighboring barstools. They witnessed part of Hitler's Beer Hall Putsch that night — half-dressed Otto and Fritz, a barely dressed pair of sisters, all four of them on their knees and peering beneath the window shades of the girls' apartment when the shooting started. Otto traveled as I did, servicing the clients of our family's magnesite mine. Fritz was a facilities inspector in the Abwehr, making sure that German army intelligence was prepared for whatever Hitler had coming. For a long time, they tried to mesh their travel schedules for a yearly meetup or two. But by the late 1930s, it had been a long time since the last pair of sisters. Fritz was working secretly against the Nazis at that point, and his rivals in the Gestapo had suspicions, and Otto, well, he got caught in the proverbial crossfire between Fritz and his rivals one night in Cologne. A lot of other shit happened, but Fritz and I had been bonded together — sometimes loosely but now tighter — ever since. He had been my guardian angel and ally, and he also had used me for his purposes. He had been my confidante, my friend, but also my boss.

And now, this note.

Now, this O with three lines drawn beneath.

I sat there on the toilet and looked at some of the graffiti in the stall. There was a drawing of the truly exceptional breasts of someone named Ludmilla, and there was the claim that someone named Ilsa's back door was "always wide fucking open." The obligatory image of an enormous penis was scratched into the paint on the door itself, and there were other a few other half-visible assertions that the cleaners had managed to obscure. One of those was missing most of the words, with the only readable bits involving "dild," "assh," and "itoris." All in all, it was pretty pedestrian shit. You wouldn't hang any of it in the Louvre, or in the Louvre's toilet.

Then I looked at the note again.

Why the hell did Fritz come to Tallinn?

I mean, I hadn't asked him to come. I hadn't been in contact with him since I left Vienna. Grimm the asshole was my handler, and that's how I dealt with things, through him. That's how Fritz wanted it on this assignment, and I followed orders. Well, except for the not getting involved with any local women who weren't prostitutes, and the not spying on the NKVD/MVD/Whatever-the-hell to help a civilian with a personal problem. Other than that, I had been good as gold — and besides, it wasn't as if Fritz would have had any way of knowing about Linna or about what I was doing for Artur.

So, why did he come?

It was all I could think about the rest of the day as I worked on a small bunch of stopgap deliveries for bars that had sold more vodka than anticipated over the weekend. We always had a few on Mondays — an extra case here or there — and all I thought about was Fritz while I knocked them out.

I actually drove three blocks past one of the deliveries before I realized I had been daydreaming about Fritz Ritter, and about the O with three lines drawn beneath it. Another time, a half-hour later, I nearly rammed into the back of a taxi because my mind was somewhere else. I was this close to plowing into the cab, and the driver knew it from the rear-view mirror. And then, while I listened to him cursing me out, I started laughing — which pissed him off even more, leading to gesticulating to go along with the cursing.

There no way I could explain to him that I wasn't laughing at him, but at the memory of something Otto used to like to say when he was teaching me how to cheat on my expenses.

"God bless the man who invented taxi cabs," is what Otto said, showing me where to add my fictions to the expense sheet.

27

I was early, and so was Fritz. I was sitting on one of the random benches along the path that led to and from the Kiek in de Kok, and I saw Fritz making his way up the hill before he saw me. I stood up to greet him and I hugged him, something I wasn't sure I'd ever done before. I still don't know why.

"Just a tourist taking in the sites?" I said.

We sat down, and he pointed at the Kiek in de Kok, outlined in the moonlight. The artillery tower really did look like a dick with a few window slots from which to fire at the invading infidels.

"You think they knew?" Fritz said.

"Knew what?"

"The whole kok double-entendre when they named it?"

"Only if they had a sense of humor."

"What are the odds?"

"Estonians, from what I've seen, don't do a whole bunch of laughing about anything," I said. "It's not a sunny place, it seems to me — not literally or figuratively. Then again, they've spent a long time getting it in the teeth from the Soviets, and then the Germans, and then the Soviets again, so..."

I didn't finish the thought, and Fritz didn't jump in with any thoughts of his own. I could take the silence for about five seconds.

"So, what the fuck are you doing here?" I said.

"And it's nice to see you, too."

"Cut the crap."

"Okay, be that way. I'm here to reassure you about the Forest Brother. I talked to Grimm—"

"Gerhard Fucking Grimm, chief asshole."

"I talked to Grimm—"

"You can talk to Grimm but you can't talk to me?"

"I'm here and I'm fucking talking to you right now," Fritz said. "Now, will you just listen for a second? I check in with Grimm now and again, and he told me about your last radio message."

"You check in? Then why can't I just deal with you directly?"

"I explained that before — I've got too much else going on. Grimm is a solid handler."

"He's a solid piece of shit, and I dare you to deny it," I said.

"He's a solid handler," Fritz said, not denying it. "And I check in on all of my agents, through their handlers. Truth be told, I check in about you more than I check in on the rest."

"Because you know that Grimm is a fucking—"

"Enough," Fritz said. "I check in with him. He told me about your message. And I'm here to tell you that it's important you stick with it. Grimm doesn't know I'm here, and he'd go crazy if he found out. I mean, screw him, I'm his boss, but he'd still go ballistic."

"But?"

"But, I'm here," Fritz said. "I'm here and I'm telling you that you need to keep pushing this guy."

We were both quiet then for a little bit. The truth was, I had no doubt that Fritz had my back. In an odd way, he had become a replacement for Otto in my life — not in the same way but, well, in some way.

"So, what questions do you have?" Fritz said.

"Nothing really about my plan, my tactics," I said. "Except, of course, if I can't convince the freaking freak to come with me. I mean, what's the answer then? Do I just poleax the giraffe and call it a day?"

We talked back and forth about what I had done, and Fritz said it all sounded fine — ingenious, even. He worried a little about Rikkart — "Might the kid become a complication?" — but I assured him that I wasn't going to allow him to get in any deeper than he was, and that there was little danger to him or the operation.

"Okay, then, anything else?" Fritz said.

"The whole backstory?" I said. "You've checked it?"

"As best as we can. Hansi Brugmann, we've seen the report from the prison in Hamburg that he was hanged. We don't have anybody on the ground there, but it looks legit. We've see that, and we've seen the interview notes where Brugmann talks about the Forest Brother and about the massacre of the Jews."

I didn't say anything, so Fritz kept going.

"We've analyzed it, and—"

"We?"

"I ran it up the flagpole."

"To Gehlen himself?"

"That's more than you need to know," Fritz said. "You know there's a chain of command and, well, leave it at that. But we all agreed that it holds together. Given that, it makes it a priority to get this Karl Tamm out of the forest and out of Estonia. The Soviets really would love to get their hands on that kind of information, just for the propaganda value. They're desperately trying to get the Baltics to like them—"

"Even as they're stealing their people and their industries, and collectivizing their farms, and just jamming it up their asses at every turn," I said.

"Which is why they would love something like this massacre story. World opinion might turn a few degrees, and everybody might be distracted a bit, and the Estonians, well..."

"You do know that the Estonians are probably split down the middle when it comes to the Nazis vs. Soviets question, don't you?" I said. "I mean, for every person horrified by the idea of Jews buried in a mass grave with saplings planted over it, there's probably another..."

Fritz put up his hand. I stopped.

"I hear you," he said. "We all know that the Estonians aren't necessarily the biggest fans of the Jews. I get that, we all get it. But not being a fan is one thing, and thinking mass slaughter is fine-and-dandy is another thing altogether. I mean, come on. They're still human beings. The people buried under the saplings were still their neighbors — well, some of them. We think most of them arrived by train from other places — almost all of them, actually — but that's not the issue. These Estonian people today are human beings with human emotions and human instincts, and if the Soviets tell them about the hundreds of Jewish bodies buried beneath those trees..."

I got it. He was right. Even if Karl Tamm scared the hell out of me, I needed to keep working him. It was the right thing geopolitically to get his freakish ass into custody, and it was the right thing, period.

"Okay, okay," I said. "You win. You and fucking Grimm. Congratulations."

We sat on the bench for about 10 more minutes, talking

about Vienna and whatnot. Then Fritz looked at his watch and stood up.

"So soon?" I said.

"My boat back to Stockholm leaves in an hour," he said. "And I have to tell you, it's a beauty. I had to piss in a bucket on the way over."

"First class, all the way."

"I'm too old for this shit," he said. Then, this time, it was him who hugged me.

PART III

28

The beat-to-hell Saab drove surprisingly well, and the engine was quieter than I had a right to expect — not brand-new quiet, but quiet enough. When I was following Krutov, I never felt as if there was anything about the car itself that might give me away.

I bought a sandwich and a newspaper and waited in the car, about a block from Patarei Prison and with a full view of the gate. The higher-ranking NKVD guys all drove black Volvos, and given that there were six of them in the prison lot when I walked out of the warehouse, that complicated my observation. But I did have Krutov's tag number, and there was a very bright light at the gate, and the Volvo drivers all tended to pause and say something to the guy in the guard shack, so I was pretty confident.

I used the newspaper mostly as a camouflage device if a car left the prison and drove in my direction — but that only happened three times in about an hour and a half. Mostly, I just ate the sandwich and processed my meeting with Fritz Ritter and worked through my conflicting feelings.

I worked for an intelligence organization that had cozied up to the Americans, and was being at least partially funded by the Americans. It didn't take a genius to see that the Gehlen Organization was putting down roots in West Germany, with a headquarters outside of Munich and all of the key people being Germans. It just made sense that Gehlen wanted us to be an essential arm of American intelligence, supplying information from the countries in the East that were now under Stalin's thumb. What might be coming down the road, I had no idea — nor did I wonder about it very often. I had become a very short-term thinker through the war years with the Resistance, and very task-oriented. See the bridge; blow up the bridge. See the Nazi colonel; shoot the Nazi colonel.

All in all, I agreed with the need to keep tabs on the Communists and to check their spread. That was true, even though I fought with Communists in the French Resistance, many Communists — mostly because they were the only fighters worth a shit, the only people willing to actively fight the Nazi occupation of France. And if I was ambivalent about my current situation — and I was, just a little — the reason was the personal experiences and the comradeship I had felt in France.

Mostly, though, I got it: Commies, bad. And in the case of Karl Tamm — my assignment and my freak — I understood the need to get him out, to prevent the Soviets from finding out about the massacre and gaining a propaganda advantage. I understood it when Grimm told me the first time, and I understood it when Fritz told me on that bench near the Kiek in de Kok.

I also appreciated, the more I thought about it, Fritz's decision to go behind Grimm's back and to tell me personally. It was an acknowledgment that he had put me in a bad situation with that asshole. It was an apology without him actually apologizing. It wasn't perfect — I mean, he could have pulled my ass out of Tallinn and taken me on the piss-in-a-bucket boat back to

Stockholm — but it wasn't nothing. And I did appreciate it, and I did value my relationship with Uncle Otto's old running buddy. All in all, I felt better about things, which I guess was the purpose of Fritz's visit. He was a good boss and a good friend.

I was thinking about all of that, my mind drifting here and there, even to picturing what those two sisters might have looked like when Otto and Fritz were watching the Beer Hall Putsch from behind the window blinds, when I saw the headlights. Another car was coming out of the prison parking. It was one of the black Volvos and, like the ones before, it stopped beneath the floodlights at the gate and the driver said something to the soldier in the guard shack. The light was strong, and the license tag was lit up just fine. It was about 7.30, and it was Krutov.

I waited maybe five seconds and then pulled out my parking spot. Even at that, I was coming up right behind Krutov very quickly. I tried to hold back, but not too far because I was afraid of losing him. The truth was, I really didn't know what I was doing. I had received plenty of instruction along the way about how to tail someone on foot and how to spot a tail, but cars were a different animal. There wasn't a ton of traffic on the streets of Tallinn — petrol scarcity was still a thing, at least occasionally — and the streets, especially in the older part of town, were narrow and short. Every two or three blocks, you needed to make another turn. If you were headed east, say, and traveling a mile through the Old Town, you would come to the end of the street, make a left and then a quick right in order to continue heading in the same direction — and you would do it four times in that mile. Each turn was another invitation for Krutov to spot me.

So, I held back with each left turn/right turn maneuver, just a few seconds, and it seemed to work well enough. I mean, I guessed I would find out at the end. He likely had a radio in the car, and if he thought he was being followed, Krutov would have little trouble arranging for a few drawn pistols in black trench coats to be waiting for me at the destination.

So, I worried about that as I drove. But I concluded something else about midway through: that Krutov wasn't driving to his house. And if I was frightened about what might be waiting in my immediate future if my surveillance skills were shit, the prospect of putting another pin in the map excited me. All I had were Krutov's home and workplace, and the idea of a third location would increase my options by 50 percent. I still had no idea about how I might neutralize Krutov when it came to threatening Artur, but creating options was, well, it was my best option at the moment. In the absence of a genius plan, a more complete map might trigger something.

At the next left turn/right turn I hung back even longer than I had been doing. After he made the right I counted to five before I followed him with my own right turn. I hadn't seen the street sign, concentrating on the one-two-three-four-five in my head, but we were in a residential neighborhood. There was a little corner store when I made the turn, but then it was just houses, modest but neat enough. At least, that's how they looked in the dark.

Krutov was about 500 feet in front of me, maybe a little less, when his brake lights shone red and he pulled over to the curb. I shut of my lights and eased into a parking spot of my own. It was less than 500 feet, more like 300. I reached into my pocket and fingered the pistol, in case Krutov started walking in my direction.

He slammed his car door and did start walking my way. Christ. I took the gun out of my pocket fingered the safety. Krutov was coming my way. I meant it when I told Artur that I wasn't an assassin, but I would absolutely kill Krutov if he had spotted me, or if I sensed any real threat or personal danger.

Krutov kept walking toward me. My window was open and I could actually hear his faint footsteps in the night. At about 250 feet, though, he turned up the front walk of a house and banged on the door. Seconds later, the porch light flicked on, and he went inside.

I was too far away to see the house number, but just as the porch light was doused, I was able to count the number of houses between me and him. Again, it was one-two-three-four-five.

29

I waited about two minutes, debating what to do, but not really. I knew I was going to get a closer look at the house, and I knew I was going to bring the tiny camera that was in the glove box. The two minutes were mostly for screwing up my courage, but again, not really. The momentum of my adrenaline was in charge, and it was carrying me to the house.

I closed the Saab door as quietly as I could, and looked up and down the street as I walked over the sidewalk. The night was dark and the street was deserted. So far, so good.

I walked the one-two-three-four-five houses in seconds. They were all identical, except for the color of their window shutters and doors: more wide than tall, probably with only one floor of living space and maybe some kind of attic or loft above. There was about 10 feet of side yard surrounding each house — so, 20 feet between houses, give or take.

I walked past the house that Krutov entered and then, at the end of the block, I doubled back. There were two lights on, both on the right side of the house. On my return trip, I scurried up the small hill of grass that led to the side yard, trying to be careful not to trip over anything in the dark or step into a hole. Because it was pretty dark. There were the lights on in the two windows of the house where Krutov was, but blinds lowered to about three-quarters length obscured most of it. The house next door was completely dark.

The windows of the house were just a bit too high to look into. I looked around for something to stand on, but there was nothing. Checking behind me, at the darkened neighbor's house, I spotted a stray cinderblock propped up against the foundation. It would do.

I brought it across the 20 feet of side yards and placed it beneath the first lit window, the one closest to the front of the house. I stepped on it and was reasonably confident I wouldn't be seen, given the dark backdrop from the house next door.

I didn't need to stand completely on tip-toes to see into the closed window, but I did need to strain just a little to see over the window jamb. Inside, across the room, was an older man dozing in a wing chair, and that was pretty much it. It was the front parlor of the house, and it was sparely decorated, and there was the man and his nap. He was dressed as a civilian, not a soldier, but that was the only observation I made.

I climbed down and picked up the cinderblock, skipping the darkened window and proceeding to the second lit window, which was at the back of the house. It was the same as the first, with the shade pulled down three-quarters of the way, but with one difference: the window was open about six inches, which meant I didn't need to strain to see over the door jamb.

It was a bedroom. There was a bed, and a chest of drawers, and a naked man propped up on a couple of pillows and stroking himself. It was Krutov.

I reached for the camera from my pocket and, as quietly as I could, I rested it on the window sill. But that wasn't the time for the first picture. First of all, what he was doing was embarrassing, yes, but only embarrassing. How he would explain to his wife about doing it in somebody else's house would be an interesting conversation, but not enough. It isn't as if he was breaking the law. I mean, if he was, it was a crime that would incarcerate the entirety of humanity

So I waited, doing my best not to watch. I waited for only about 30 seconds, as it turned out. That's when the bedroom door opened, and the two girls walked in.

And they really were girls. They were wearing makeup — lipstick and too much rouge on their cheeks — but they looked to be as old as Krutov's daughters, 12 to 14. They could have been schoolmates. But these two weren't laughing at some joke outside of church. They were standing there with frilly nightgowns covering their bodies, pink lace and dead eyes. There was nothing the makeup could do about the dead eyes. They would be what haunted me for weeks.

Part of me couldn't believe how angry I felt, but that wasn't the part that was in control of my actions. I was an observer, not a participant, and I knew I wasn't going to be a participant. It was like Leon used to tell me when he was a police reporter in Vienna. He said, "By your second or third murder, you find yourself able to take notes about the color of the stiff's suit or the fact that his hat lay upside down on the sidewalk. That the guy is dead, and what that might mean to his family and friends, never crosses you mind. All you're doing is taking notes, describing the street corner, trying not to step in his blood."

That was me, standing on that cinderblock. But I wasn't taking notes. I was doing the quick mental calculation about when to snap the first picture. Because while the camera truly was a marvel, so small and with such good picture quality, there still was a light click when you took the picture. Advancing the film between shots also made noise, but I could lower the camera below the open window and confidently muffle that. It was the click, though, that I couldn't predict. I wasn't 10 feet away from the bed, after all.

I wanted to wait for some conversation to fill the stillness. At the same time, I knew I needed to get the girls' faces, needed to get them clear. Their age needed to be unmistakable if this was to have its maximum effect — because, again, an NKVD agent caught with a couple of hookers would be embarrassing, but maybe not embarrassing enough.

It was when Krutov said, "You can take them off," that I snapped the first picture.

It was after they were naked, and Krutov said, "You remember, like the last time," that I snapped the second picture.

It was after the three of them were entangled, and Krutov continued offering instructions, that I snapped the third and fourth and fifth pictures. That's when the wave of sadness hit me, and I was ready to be done — because of the sadness, and because I knew that odds of getting away undetected grew smaller with each click.

But then the bedroom door opened again. A third child walked in — or, rather, was shoved in by an unseen arm. This one was completely naked. This one was a boy. Again, maybe 12 years old. Again, dead eyes. He reached down and grabbed himself, and walked over to the bed. I took one more picture before he joined in, hoping that I captured his face, so young, so terrified. And then I hopped down off of the cinderblock, unable to watch anymore.

If the pictures came out okay, I had Krutov where I needed him to be if Artur was to avoid being blackmailed. And that, I had to admit, excited me even as the rest of it disgusted me. There were still things to work out — the approach to Krutov most of all — but this was a success, however awful.

The half-bottle of vodka I drank that night, trying to induce sleep, was a multi-faceted anesthetic, then — a quarter-bottle to quell my adrenaline, a quarter-bottle to obliterate my revulsion.

30

Thursday night in The Lantern, again.

Mayhem again, fueled by alcohol and testosterone.

I got my first beer from Tuule behind the bar, and she acted as if she barely knew me, like shit on her shoe that she only vaguely remembered stepping in. So, there was that. I took a lap around and didn't see Rikkart, so I settled into a two-person booth on the far side that was empty. It was still early, and based on my first visit, the mayhem would multiply within about an hour.

I had spent almost the entire drive from Tallinn thinking about Krutov. I knew I wasn't an assassin, but nobody in possession of the facts would blame me for shooting him. Even though I didn't know exactly what kind of place that house was — open to fucking perverts of every perverted stripe, or just to NKVD men, or just to Krutov — it didn't really matter. Robbing kids of their childhood is criminal theft. It should be punishable by death.

But I wasn't going to shoot him in cold blood. I knew that. Since I had pretty much woken up and gotten straight on the road, I hadn't told Artur about what I had. I also hadn't developed the photographs yet. I just didn't have the stomach for it but I promised myself I would after this trip to Tartu, after I got Karl Tamm's freakish ass into my car and into hiding as we waited for Antti's boat ride to Helsinki. Saturday, maybe Sunday, I'd have the pictures and talk to Artur about a plan.

It was only in the last few miles that I was able to focus on Tamm. The more I thought about it, about the details, the more concerned I became about what I needed to pull it off. It was what I was brooding about when I saw Rikkart and his friends enter the bar and buy their first from Tuule. Mugs in hand, the friends headed to an empty booth on the other side, but Rikkart came straight to me.

"How did you—"

"Tuule told me," he said.

"And what did she call me?"

"Word for word, 'Your asshole fucking uncle is over there.' So, you obviously made a good impression."

"That's good?"

"Trust me, that's good. So, what's the good news, Uncle Alex?"

"Cut it out."

"But you are fucking my cousin Linna, and she's kind of like my aunt, and besides—"

"Enough," I said. But I wasn't mad. Despite the age difference, my conversations with Rikkart reminded me of my conversations with Leon, back when we were in our twenties, before Hitler and the second war, before most of real life had intruded upon our immature asshole bullshit.

The last thing I wanted to do was rob Rikkart of a minute of his own immature asshole bullshit phase of life. But as I kept going over it in my head in the Saab during the drive to Tartu, and in the bar before he arrived, I just didn't see another way.

"Listen—"

"I can get a gun," Rikkart said. It was as if he was reading my mind, but I was still stunned and I reacted like I was stunned.

"Wait a minute—"

"Fuck you, Uncle. You know you were about to ask me."

"I... I..."

"Cat got your tongue? I'm sure that Tulle hopes that isn't the case. Probably cousin Linna, too."

"Listen," I said, gathering myself. "Sometimes, you're too smart for your own good. That's what I'm worried about."

"I assume you have a gun, but I'm sure you think you need another one, just in case," he said. "Or somebody to drive back to Tallinn. I mean, even if that hideous motherfucker is cooperative, well..."

"You never know," I said, more to myself than to Rikkart. "You never know."

We both took long sips from our beers. Mine was done, and Rikkart chugged the remainder of his and grabbed the mugs. "My treat," he said, heading for the bar.

As I watched him, I thought about it and couldn't believe what I was doing. Putting a civilian kid, Linna's cousin, into the middle of this thing was equal parts selfish and irresponsible. I knew that intellectually, but I also didn't see any other way.

He came back with the beers, and we both took long pulls. And then I said, "There's something else."

"What?"

"I really need another guy."

"And another gun?" Rikkart said.

"Just to be sure. One of you drives, the other rides shotgun, and I cram into the backseat with the gorilla/giraffe. Can you get your buddy Leks from the other night?"

"He'd probably do it for free."

"My impression is, he does nothing for free."

"Come to think of it, you're right."

"I'll double what I paid you the last time for delivering the message, in advance," I said. Then I reached into my pocket and counted from a roll of bills.

"Holy fuck," Rikkart said, fanning the cash.

"Beer for the semester," I said.

"More like tuition for the semester," he said.

I talked him through the logistics, as I saw them, for the meet the next afternoon. He listened, nodded, asked a smart question. I felt decent about the whole thing, even as I felt like a complete shithead.

"One other thing — handcuffs," I said. "I mean, I guess I could use a rope, but—"

"Not a problem."

I asked a question with my eyes.

"For all I know, Leks has some already," Rikkart said. "And, if he doesn't, I'm sure he can get some from the brothel where he has his special arrangement."

"Really now? And what do you know about whorehouses and handcuffs?"

"Hey, I hear things," he said. At which point, he stuffed the money in his pocket and rejoined his buddies in their booth across the way.

I spent the rest of the night drinking at the same bar seat where I had spent the previous night. And, as it turned out, Rikkart was right about Tuule. It was the same as that first night: stack the chairs, mop the floor, only a lick and a promise, et cetera. Except, this time, there was a second et cetera in the morning.

31

The Rock remained The Rock — smelly, grimy, all of that. Seeing as how I hadn't done a careful study the time before, other than being overwhelmed by their odor, I couldn't be sure if the three men at the bar were the same three men. The stench was the same, though.

I bought three beers and pointed again to the little nook with the half-height swinging doors.

"Knock yourself out," the bartender said. He could not have been less interested.

We took up our same positions — me inside the nook, Rikkart at the table outside. The difference this time was that Rikkart also was carrying a pistol, a tiny .22 caliber thing whose bullets might not pierce the bushy black hair on Karl Tamm's chest — assuming, that is, that his chest hair was as thick and unruly as the hair on his face and on his head. I swear, it was like you were looking at a cat's eyes in a dark room when you talked to him.

"Nice lady gun," I said, when Rikkart showed it to me.

"It'll do."

"And you know that how, exactly?"

"It'll fucking do, Uncle."

"Have you ever fired it?"

"At some tin cans."

"Did it at least knock them off the fence?"

"It'll do, Uncle," he said. And, the truth was, he was right. If we were in a position where Rikkart was actually firing the thing, the whole situation would have devolved into such a mess that stunning Tamm would likely be plenty good enough. And my instructions were clear — repeated often enough that Rikkart mocked me by reciting them from memory.

"Remember," I said.

"And I quote," he said, taking on a lousy imitation of my voice. "'If he's completely out of control, and if you're saving my life or your life, blast away. But whatever happens, after you fire that fucking thing, you run. You empty it and you fucking run. Promise me.'"

He did promise me, four or five times. Beside Rikkart being armed, there were two other differences in our setup. One was Leks, who was sitting out front in the driver's seat of the Saab, also armed, also with a lady gun, his borrowed from one of the actual ladies at the brothel. His job was to be the driver on the trip back to Tallinn, but also to be a lookout. If he saw any other Forest Brothers entering the bar, he was to follow them in.

The other difference was the handcuffs.

"Where'd you get them?"

"Leks got them from the brothel," Rikkart said.

I picked them up and sniffed them.

"Don't smell any of the girls' perfume," I said.

"They're mostly for the men, not the girls."

I arched an eyebrow.

"I mean, I hear things," Rikkart said.

I went into the nook and sat down and sipped my beer. Five

minutes later, Tamm came through the swinging doors, right on time.

It was the same as the last time. Before we talked, Tamm downed his beer in two and the remains of my beer in one. When I walked to the swinging doors, Rikkart was already at the bar, and he brought over two more beers within seconds. Tamm drank half of that one, belched loud enough for the sleeping men at the bar to hear, and then began talking.

"I'm interested," he said.

"Good."

"But I'm still worried."

"About what?"

"This is my fucking life now, asshole. I've done good work here."

"Yeah, the Russians are really fucking scared of you. They're all running back to Moscow. Let's go out on the road and watch them — it's a convoy."

"Fuck you," Tamm said, and then his eyes fell, and then he finished his beer and snatched mine from my hands. I had debated whether or not to play the humiliation card, and decided, what the hell. Because the truth was, almost all of the Forest Brothers had been rounded up by the Soviet army. Tamm and whoever was left really were dead-enders who were accomplishing nothing. They were proving a point that had become meaningless to everyone but themselves. They had to know it, too — and when I shoved it in Tamm's face, and his eyes fell, I could tell for sure that he did know it.

"Look," I said. "This is a way out for you. And it's a meaningful way out. There's a fight to be continued, and if you get back with Hansi Brugmann, it will be a fight that is organized, and equipped, and well-thought-out, and well-funded. It'll be a better fight and it'll be a better life. I mean, you won't be picking pine needles out of your crotch hair after fucking whores in the forest anymore."

"You know, I had a wife," he said. It took every bit of self-control to keep me from replying, "A blind woman is she?"

Instead, I said, "Maybe still."

Tamm waved his hand. Over his shoulder, Rikkart was looking over the half-doors and holding two more beers. He asked, with his eyes, how things were going. I answered, also with my eyes, okay.

Tamm began on his next beer and I decided to just let him think for a minute.

Then he said, "I need more time. I need another week."

"What the fuck, Karl?" I said, probably louder than I intended. He was stunned by the volume, or maybe it was my use of his name. I wasn't sure, but I think it was the first time I had called him Karl.

"It's my fucking life, asshole," he said, the first time defiantly, the second time quietly. I slid my beer across the table to him and said, "Be right back — gotta piss."

Through the swinging doors and into the main bar, I nodded at Rikkart and headed for the toilet. We had worked this out ahead of time. If I headed to the toilet, he was to go outside and get Leks. It meant that things were not going swimmingly, and that there was a chance we would be capturing Tamm rather than escorting him.

Once they were in place, we had worked out what to do. If they heard a commotion in the nook, they were to come in and we would see if we could subdue the gorilla/giraffe. No guns, though. Not yet. Other than that, they were to wait and see — and they were not to pull their pistols until they saw me pull mine first.

"'Pull mine?'" Rikkart had said, and then giggled, when I first sketched it out.

"Fucking child."

"Whatever you say, Uncle."

I really did have to piss, as it turned out, or maybe it was just my military experience: eat when you can, shit when you can, piss when you can, sleep when you can. I wasn't sure what to do about Tamm. He wasn't belligerent, not at all. In fact, he was kind of morose. I had gotten to him — of that, I was pretty sure. I was giving him a way out of a shitty life, and he knew it. I was giving him a chance to return to what he saw as his glory days under Hansi Brugmann, the Jew-killer, and he knew that, too. What the hesitation was about, I wasn't sure. It was probably just human inertia — either that or he was worried about disappointing the other Forest Brothers still in hiding.

Part of me really did just want to fucking shoot him — to come back from the toilet, and put two slugs in the back of his head while he drank my beer, and be done with it. It really would accomplish what Grimm wanted to accomplish — to silence Tamm. That was really the goal, stripped of the niceties: to keep the last participant in the massacre of Jews in Kalevi from blabbing about it to the Soviets, to make sure that the Soviet would not gain that propaganda victory.

And, well, who was I kidding? I insisted to Artur that I wasn't an assassin, but, come on. I killed those two soldiers guarding the NKVD headquarters, and I had killed plenty more in France. Many more. And if I liked to think that I only did it to defend myself, or when absolutely necessary, or because I was a soldier in a war, well, let's just say that I didn't re-examine the past details very often, just in case I was wrong about myself.

But there was another matter as well. There were two matters, actually — Rikkart and Leks. If I went back to the nook and started blasting away, I could just make a run for it back to Tallinn and likely get away with it. Rikkart and Leks, though, lived in Tartu. They weren't going to be able to run anywhere.

And even if the bartender truly appeared not to give a shit about anything, well, he still had eyes. And there would be cops. And while the two of them might be fine, it was a question. It was a real question and a real complication of taking them on as my accomplices.

The truth was, I knew I wasn't going to shoot Tamm unless I had to shoot him. I knew that when I walked out of the toilet, and detoured at the bar for two more beers, and saw that Leks had joined Rikkart at the table outside of the nook.

I put one of the beers in front of Tamm and sipped from the other.

"If it's your friends in there that you're worried about," I said.

"They're not my friends — they're my fucking brothers, asshole," he said.

"Whatever you call them, you are continuing the struggle if you rejoin Hansi Brugmann."

"Whatever you call them," he said, mocking me. "'Brothers' is what I call them because brothers is what they are. That means something. And if you're such a piece of shit that you can't realize it..."

He stopped again and drank from the mug. When it was empty, he grabbed my mug.

"I'm coming with you he said."

Long drink.

"But I need more time."

"Fuck me."

"Yeah, fuck you," Tamm said. "I need more time. I need another week. But I will come with you. You have my word. Same time, next week, and we'll do it."

"But," I said, beginning one final counter argument that quicker was better, and that good-byes were only going to make it harder, and including the phrase "just ripping off the bandage."

"This isn't a fucking bandage," Tamm said. "These are my brothers."

Then, louder: "Brothers."

Then, quieter, "You really are a piece of shit. I mean, are you even a human being?"

It took all of my self-control to keep from replying, "Said the bastard child of a gorilla and a giraffe."

But I said nothing. I just nodded, and then Tamm pushed back his chair and barged through the swinging doors. I followed behind. Rikkart and Leks were wide-eyed, their hands in their pockets, undoubtedly fingering their lady guns.

I went to the bar, got three more beers, and sat down and explained.

32

—————

Linna had picked the lock into my apartment and was naked on the couch when I returned from Tartu, half dozing beneath a wool blanket. The sex was quick and mechanical. We split a beer as we got dressed.

"Where—" she said.

I put up my hand to avoid the question and, hopefully, the conversation.

"Look, it's your life and you've told me a little, and I guess that's enough," she said. "I mean, I don't let anybody get close, so I can't expect my more from anyone else. It's just..."

Linna stopped, searching for the phrase.

"I don't know," she said. "You just seem distracted, and not in a good way. Not the distractions of a happy, busy life. Or, not the distractions of the life you sketched out for me, of the end of grieving for a dead wife and child. Those kinds of things, I've seen before. I understand them. And maybe I'm wrong, and that's all this is, but your preoccupation seems different. More, I don't know, more dark."

I fumfered a couple of words, then stopped. Christ, how to answer this? Not with the truth, obviously. Not with a cavalcade of stories about a Nazi-loving freak who hides in the forest, and dead soldiers in the alley outside NKVD headquarters, and dead eyes. God, those dead eyes.

So, I said, "No, it's just what I told you before. I can't explain it. I mean, I thought I was over it all — and, really, I am mostly over it all. But going back and seeing their graves, it triggered something deep inside. And now, I feel like, if I make the decision that this visit will be the last visit, that it will be over in a way that... Fuck, I don't know. But that's it."

I listened to myself say the words and couldn't believe how real I sounded, what an artful liar I had become. It scared me in some ways, to be honest.

Linna nodded, and flicked a finger at the corner of her eye. And then we just sat there, shucking on our pants, tying our shoes. But, even as well as the lie had landed, I was worried. First was my concern that all of my activities, official and unofficial, clever and grotesque, were showing on my face — because I really did pride myself on my ability to project an even mood and temperament, regardless of the shitstorm over the next hill. If I wasn't fooling Linna, that was a significant problem.

Because, the truth was, I didn't think I was outwardly any different. But if she was able to pick up on subtle clues, barely discernible tics, then Linna and I had grown too close. How fuck-food-finis had evolved into too close, I had no idea — because I really didn't feel close to her. I mean, she had told me the story of her father, and brought me to see her mother, and I did feel something for what she had been through. But close? Really close? No, not from my end. But, well, that seemed to be the reality.

On the most mundane level, it was bad spy craft, first of all. If Fritz had said it once, he'd said it 20 times: "Whores only." There was a reason he said it, and this was it.

But it was more than that, more complicated. When Manon

and I met and fell in love and got married, we both were intelligence professionals — me for the Czechs, her for France. I did not drag her into the French Resistance — more the opposite, probably. And when she and our unborn child died, I knew it wasn't my fault but I also knew that my actions were tangled up in everything that happened. And, the truth was, it had been years since I had tortured myself by trying to do the untangling.

There was nothing I could have done to prevent Manon from getting involved in, well, in all of it. But Linna, I couldn't allow her to become another tangle in my dark life. I couldn't have her grow too close for that reason, a personal reason. Not tradecraft — a personal reason. I couldn't let her get close because I didn't want close. I didn't want that ever again — not for me, not for any woman.

33

_____

I told Linna I would meet her at the warehouse in about two hours. She had some kind of fire to put out — as she put it, it had to do with "the fucking piece of shit bottle cleaners" — and I told her I'd get a head start on the delivery schedule for the upcoming week.

As soon as she left, I pulled out the suitcase from under the bed that contained the portable darkroom equipment. It was a pretty easy process — mix the chemical bath, put the blackout curtain over the bathroom window, screw in the red light bulb, and get to work. As it turned out, the camera really was a fine piece of machinery. The pictures from Krutov's, well, I didn't even know what to call it, were more than clear enough. It was all there for anyone who cared to see — Krutov, the two girls, then the boy. And the dead eyes — but only in one of the pictures, one with one of the girls.

After the photos were dry, I wrapped them in a homemade envelope made out of newspaper and drove to the warehouse. When I got inside, I was more than 100 feet from Linna's office but I could hear her yelling, probably into the telephone — not the words, not except for the occasional "fuck," just the tone. I put the newspaper envelope at the bottom of the forms on my clipboard and worked on the delivery schedules. I had to wait for Linna to finish yelling and go home, leaving only Artur in the adjacent office. Because Artur was always there on Saturday, making sure the books balanced.

After about a half-hour, Linna did storm out, and I went in to see Artur. He looked borderline catatonic. He saw me in the doorway and just said, "Oh, fuck." He held up a small envelope, and I reached over and snatched it from his shaking hand.

The message was short and to the point:

Sunday night, 8 p.m., St. Catherine's Passage. I'll explain our new arrangement then.

Krutov

"Well, that's it, then," Artur said.

"Cheer up, asshole."

I pulled out the newspaper envelope from the bottom of the clipboard and slid them across the desk. As he was unwrapping the photographs, I said, "Look, this is some sick shit, but it'll work for you."

Artur opened the packet and looked at the photos, one by one. He started with a clinical manner, but about halfway through, he was blinking away tears and kind of looking at them side-eyed, as if turning his head a little and squinting would prevent the images from being etched on his subconscious forever.

When he was done with the last photo, he turned the stack upside down on the desk — again, as if that would hide what he had just seen.

"With these, you'll be able to..." I said.

"Blackmail him," he said.

I nodded. Artur just sat there, elbows on the desk. A few

seconds later, he slumped back in the desk chair. He was not acting like a person whose problems had been solved.

Ten seconds, more.

Then, "Fuck it," he said. "If you get me a gun, I'll kill him myself."

"Easy, cowboy," I said.

"Sick bastard."

"No doubt."

"He doesn't deserve to live."

"I don't disagree."

"Then I'll shoot him."

"It's not that easy."

"It's easy as hell," he said. "You just pull the trigger. It's not like he'll be bringing a posse with him to work out the deals of extorting some random homo."

"You don't know that," I said. "You don't know anything about this guy."

"Other than that he's the sickest bastard—"

"Agreed," I said. "No question about it. No need for argument. But this is about you right now, and keeping you safe. Everything else has to be secondary."

"Fuck secondary. You get me a pistol, and I'll fucking kill him, and I'll be safer than safe."

"Unless some busybody walking their dog sees you or hears the shot. Unless he has somebody waiting for him in the car. Unless, shit, you know what I'm saying."

"None of that is a fatal flaw," he said. "One shot between the eyes, and then I'm in the wind."

"No, you're being naive," I said. "I mean, come on. What if you miss? Or just graze him? Or he hits your arm, and knocks it off target, and then he grabs you, and then you're in a gunfight with a trained killer. No. No."

And then I explained the plan I had concocted in the last

couple of minutes, after Artur showed me the note from Krutov. As we leaned over the desk and I laid it out, I noticed this one time when Artur inadvertently touched the stack of upside-down photos. His hand jerked away as if he had touched a hot stove.

34

St. Catherine's Passage, not far from the Town Hall, was pretty much just an alley in the Old Town. There was St. Catherine's Church on one side and some random buildings on the other. It was cobbled and smelled vaguely of piss. There was a single bare light bulb hanging from a barely hanging fixture about a third of the way in from Vene Street. The entrance was close to the post office where Linna's father had been killed in the bombing, just across the street. That was where Artur was parked in the Saab. He was in the driver's seat, wearing my watch cap, undoubtedly trying not to soil the upholstery.

I had on a different hat and also the fake eyeglasses and a scarf wrapped loosely up to my chin. It was enough of a disguise. The way I figured it, Krutov would know quickly enough that I wasn't Artur, but I didn't want him to know from 30 feet away, either. I thought about standing in the dark but no. We were going to need the light in the end.

I arrived 15 minutes early. I fingered the photographs in my breast pocket and the pistol in my side pocket. About five minutes in, I walked a few steps from beneath the light and contributed to the vague smell of piss. Five minutes, 10 minutes, 15 minutes, and no one came through the passage.

Sixteen minutes.

Seventeen minutes.

Then I heard the footsteps. They were coming from the other end, not the one where Artur was parked. I guessed that Krutov would come from that direction, mostly because the parking was easier at that end.

I made sure to stand directly under the light, so Krutov would see me, so he wouldn't be startled by someone emerging from the shadows. Soon enough, I saw him in silhouette, and he saw me. When he was close enough, he looked at me and saw that I wasn't Krutov, and the slightest slowing of his walk while he checked me out was replaced by his normal cadence. He was walking past me, and I waited until he was about 10 feet past.

And then I said, "Krutov."

There was no question mark. It was a statement. He stopped, turned on his heel, came back and examined me up and down.

"No, not Artur," I said.

There was little doubt that Krutov was carrying a weapon, but the surprise in his eyes when I said Artur's name did not result in him reaching into either of his jacket pockets, or unbuttoning the jacket to get at a pistol in a shoulder holster. His manner was calm but his eyes were, I don't know, active. Alert. Maybe they were like that all the time — trained killer and all that.

"I have something for you to look at," I said. When I reached into my breast pocket, Krutov's right hand did move to his side pocket. So, at least I knew where he was carrying.

"Photographs," I said. When I pulled the stack out of my pocket, he took his right hand out of his pocket and accepted them.

"You'll need the light," I said, and then I stepped away from beneath the bare bulb and the barely hanging fixture, and Krutov took my place.

Again, I watched his eyes. They widened when he saw the first picture, but only a little. By the second, and the third, and the rest, his face betrayed nothing.

Then he put the photos in his left hand and reached into his pocket with his right hand and produced what was undoubtedly his standard issue NKVD pistol. And, well, let's just say that it wasn't a lady gun.

"I could shoot you right here, whoever you are," he said.

"You could, but you won't."

"You're pretty confident for a man staring down the barrel of an MVD pistol."

"NKVD, MVD, doesn't much matter to me," I said. "And you're not going to shoot me, and we both know it."

"And why not?"

"Because you don't have the negatives. And you don't have the copies. So, just put that fucking thing away and let's have a civilized conversation."

When he did, indeed, put the pistol back into his pocket, I took it for the victory that it was. My choices at that point were either to shame the fucking pervert for a while, just for fun, or to simply get on with it. I had to admit being tempted by the first, but I settled for the second.

"Besides this set — which is yours to keep, by the way — there are four sets of copies that have been printed. And then there are the negatives, of course."

"The fuck—"

"Four copies, Krutov," I said. "And the terms here are simple enough. If anything happens to me, they get sent. If you so much as get within shooting distance of Artur, or if you send him any more of those fucking notes, or if you contact him in any way, they get sent. All four copies get sent."

Krutov stood there under the dim light, thinking. It was a long think. In the middle of it, he reached out the photographs and I said, "No, like I said, they're yours." He paused for a second and shoved them into the same pocket with the pistol. Then he stood there, leaning against the stone wall now, his head half tilted up toward the bare light bulb, and thought some more.

And then, finally, he said, "Sent where?"

"Didn't hear you, Krutov."

"Sent where, asshole?"

I did my best not to grin in his face, to keep it businesslike. I pretty much succeeded, I think. Pretty much.

"One copy to your wife, obviously," I said. "The second copy to your boss in the prison — I don't know his name yet, but I'll find out easily enough. The third copy to Captain Igor Kuznetzov at Pikk 59."

"Kuznetzov? And you know him how?"

"Doesn't really matter, does it?" I said.

Krutov began to say something else and then stopped almost immediately, swallowing the first syllable. Then I waited until he asked.

"And the fourth copy?"

"Glad you asked," I said. "That one will go to the priest at St. Nicholas Church, the one where you bring your wife and those two cute girls every Sunday."

"How the..." But Krutov stopped himself almost as soon as he started. He wanted to know how I knew about his family, but it didn't really matter, and he realized it immediately. And then I couldn't resist.

Pointing to the pocket where he had stuffed the photographs, I said, "Do you think they're older or younger than your daughters?"

At that, Krutov leaned back against the wall again, and half tilted his head toward the bare bulb again. Then he closed his eyes and said, "I should just kill you and take my chances."

In truth, there weren't four copies of the photographs. There were only the negatives, mostly because I didn't have enough photographic paper to print even one more set. The negatives were in the Saab with Artur, in an envelope addressed to Captain Igor Kuznetzov at Pikk 59. Artur was under instructions that, if he heard a gunshot, he was to walk across the street to the post office and mail the envelope, and then to start the car and drive away.

"But you won't kill me," I said. "And, you know, the more I've been thinking, there might be a way out for you here. A transfer. You have enough service time, I have to imagine you could make the request."

"It's not like booking a fucking cruise," he said.

"No, I imagine not," I said. "And I imagine Tallinn isn't all that sought-after a posting if you're an agent with ambition. Then again, I have to wonder about your prospects seeing as how you didn't even get one of the good jobs in Tallinn, that they stuck you in Siberia."

"How do you know those assholes call it Siberia?"

"Because I know."

Again, Krutov's eyes closed when he leaned back.

"So, you ask for a transfer," I said. "It'll have to be someplace shitty if they're going to say yes — but it can't be so shitty that it makes no sense. Where are you from?"

"Just outside Moscow."

"Well, that's obviously out. I'm sure there are NKVD agents actually knifing each other to get a transfer to Moscow. Like, actually knifing — am I right, motherfucker?"

Krutov didn't answer.

"So, where's your wife from?" I said. "No, don't tell me."

"Fuck you."

"It's that bad, huh? Well, perfect. Does she want to go back?"

"She'd love to go back."

"So, that's it — problem solved. I'm sure it's a place where nobody volunteers to go, but you have a reason, and they'll buy it. Hell, they'll probably stamp the papers before you leave the office so you can't change your mind. And that'll be that. Artur and I won't know where you are, and we have no desire to fuck with you besides. We're playing defense here. You go away, all of this goes away."

Krutov thought one more time, but not for very long at all.

"Let's say, I don't know, 30 days," I said. "That should be enough time to get your ass transferred to wherever-the-fuck. And if you're still in Tallinn after that, we'll be in contact and you won't like it. Or, maybe we'll just start sending some of the photos to Kuznetzov — the first one with your whole face cut out, and then the next one, a few days later, with half of your face cut out, and then, you get the idea."

Krutov said nothing, which I took for assent. He threw his shoulders back, straightened his jacket, and began walking back toward where he had parked.

"Take care of those girls of yours," I said.

He paused again, just for a beat, and then he continued walking away. Krutov never turned back, not even for the quickest of glances, when I said, "Take care of them, because I know how much you love your little girls."

35

I got back to the Saab and told Artur everything. He cried when he thanked me. I told him I was about 95 percent sure that he was in the clear but that, just in case, we needed to hide the envelope with the negatives someplace where both of us would have access to it. That way, if something happened to one of us, the other could mail it to Kuznetzov. He suggested the bottom drawer of the last file cabinet in his office, and that would work fine.

"Give me a minute," I said. I got out of the car and walked across the street to Telegraaf House. Inside, I used one of the public phones and called the number I had obtained earlier.

Back in the car, I gave him a few more of the details of the conversation with Krutov. Artur punched the air — and the ceiling of the car — when I recited the last words I said to Krutov as he was walking away.

"Part of me, though—"

"I get it," I said. "Part of me, too. It's not enough punishment. It's really not a punishment at all. But I wasn't kidding. We're playing defense here, and getting him the fuck out of Tallinn, well, that's going to have to be enough."

Artur flexed his hand and examined the knuckles that had punched the roof of the Saab. He said, "So, this is the only way this whole incident has hurt me — sore fucking knuckles. God, I really don't know how to thank you."

"Well," I said, and then I began mimicking the unbuttoning of my pants.

"Mature fucking asshole," Artur said. Then, quieter, "Mature fucking asshole."

I looked at my watch. It had been 15 minutes since I had made the telephone call.

"Just drive," I said. And then I directed him along a route that I could remember without seeing the street signs, left and a quick right at the end of the street, then left and a quick right at the end of the street, then again, then again.

When we arrived at the house, the street was already crowded with police cars and flashing lights. We parked six or seven houses away and walked up the sidewalk. There was a small crowd of neighbors standing there, shivering. We joined them.

Police walked in and out of the house where Krutov, well. After a minute or two, cops escorted two men out of the front door. One of them could have been the guy who had been snoozing in the chair in the parlor when I peeked through the window, but I wasn't sure. The other one was barefoot, likely a customer.

They were thrown into the back of a wagon and driven away. Maybe a minute later, another car with more flashing lights arrived. Two lady cops got out and hustled inside. Maybe five minutes later, they came out with three kids, two girls and a boy, all of them wrapped in blankets.

I could see Artur looking at them, and I was looking at them, and then he said, "I'm not sure it's the same—"

"Me neither," I said.

The lady cops got the kids into their car and drove away. The crowd of neighbors began to thin. I could only wonder what they had seen and not seen, known and not known, with nobody notifying the police until I made that call from the post office. Anyway, after another minute or so, it was just Artur and I on the sidewalk, but neither of us seemed ready to go.

Finally, I said, "Drink?"

And, he said, "Drunk."

And then we spent the rest of the night going about the business of celebrating, and of trying to forget.

36

W hen Antti was doing legitimate business, he docked his boat at the marina with the rest. There, the skippers gassed up, and did their cleaning and maintenance, and got their paperwork stamped by the Estonian soldier-types assigned to keeping track of small craft traffic in the gulf.

He had told me that they searched the cargo sometimes, and that they weren't bribe-able. "The damndest fucking thing," he said. "They're not offended or anything when you offer, but they never take it. One time, I asked one of them why not. And, he said, "Whatever you have in your pocket isn't worth two in the back of the head from a guy in a black trench coat."

"The NKVD, or MVD, or whatever the fuck you call them," I said, and Antti nodded. "I mean, it's so funny. The NKVD takes bribes from Linna at the vodka warehouse like it was part of their job description, but if you're one of the frozen-assed Estonians on the sea patrol, forget it. And they'll kill you for it? Life really isn't fair."

"And this is just dawning on you now, Copernicus?"

"Copernicus was Polish. I'm Austrian."

"You know what I'm fucking saying," Antti said.

When I got to the marina, I found him scraping some kind of shit off of the hull of his boat.

"Barnacles," he said. "My ruination."

"Do they come off easy?"

"Do they look like they come off easy?"

"Want some help?"

"And have your amateur ass poke a hole in my side? No, thank you," he said.

I sat on the pier and watched him work for another 10 minutes before he sighed loudly and declared, "Fuck it."

"No good?"

"Better than before."

"Must have been a disaster before, because that just looks like you pushed the gravy around the plate a little."

"Said the fucking barnacle expert. Fuck."

He made some of the terrible coffee, and we sat on the deck. Before I chose my seat, I said, "Which way is downwind?"

"Good point."

He took the downwind seat, which saved me from most of his digestive incidents. After one particular blast, I said, "I mean, what the hell do you eat?"

"It's not the food. It's a family trait — you should have seen my father. Some people get royal titles passed down to them, others get the family business. This is what Antti got."

Another blast. We both laughed.

"So," he said.

"So I need to make a reservation."

"When?"

"Saturday or Sunday."

"Can't be Sunday. Got a client."

"What client?"

"Like it's any of your fucking business. I'm booked on

Sunday. It can't be changed. It can't be moved. It can't be delayed. It just can't."

I had thought it through, and there was a chance that I could do it on Friday night. That, of course, is if everything went smoothly and Karl Tamm didn't give us any trouble. The odds of that, I feared, were lower than ideal — so, Saturday was the most likely time. Of course, that meant Tamm would likely have to spend the night on my couch — after which, of course, I would have to burn the fucking thing. Only if the operation was a true disaster would Sunday come into play. That was just a precaution, and it probably wasn't really necessary. And seeing as how it wasn't possible, anyway, there was no reason to be worrying about it.

"Okay, Saturday night," I said.

"Usual place?"

I nodded. Our "usual place" was a cove about a mile south of the marina — far enough away to be secluded but close enough so it wasn't a complete pain in the ass to reach.

"Another passenger besides you?"

I nodded again.

"The Nazi giraffe?"

Another nod.

"Fuck," Antti said. "What a world we live in. What a goddamned world."

We drank our coffee, which had already gone cold. I asked him if he was available for a really quick jaunt on the great circle route that night because I needed to update Grimm with my plans by radio. Mostly, I needed him to be available to receive messages on Saturday night, to receive his gift-wrapped Nazi son of a gorilla and a giraffe soon after.

Antti was available because, as he said, "Who needs sleep when my friendly neighborhood Austrian spy is waving around wads of cash?"

When I sent the message, the reply came within two minutes:

"Message received."

It was a half-hour in and a half-hour back. He dropped me at the cove, which had a broken-down pier on one side. The two of us had actually repaired the ladder at one point, and I was stepping onto it when Antti said something that I didn't hear.

"You'll have a gun, right?"

I patted my jacket pocket and said, "You too, right?"

"Always," he said. "I mean, you never know when you're going to have to shoot a gorilla or a giraffe in the wild."

37

The next day, at about noon, there was a commotion in the warehouse. I was sitting in the delivery van and, truth be told, resting my eyes. I woke with a start when I saw what was happening, way over on the other side, over by the main entrance.

One, two, three, four, five black trench coats came in, pistols drawn. They were followed by three guys in military uniforms, carrying rifles. Nobody was really pointing a weapon at any of the warehouse workers. They were just showing the iron.

It took me two or three seconds for all of it to register. I immediately left the van and walked — walked, not ran — over the Artur's office. He had seen what was happening through the window — his office had a huge window through which he could scan the warehouse. So did Linna's office. As I reached Artur's door, she was emerging from hers and saying, "Fuck. Already?"

"Already?"

"It happens every six months or so," she said. "I don't think it's six months this time, though. I don't think it's fucking close."

"What is 'it'?"

"A raid," she said. "Another goddamned raid."

Linna went on to explain. About twice a year, her NKVD protectors from across the parking lot staged a raid in the warehouse. She said, "It's really just the first step in the renegotiation of our terms."

Twice a year, they came across the parking lot from the prison. Twice a year, they shut the distillery down.

"Look at them," Linna said. She pointed at knots of our coworkers, joking and laughing. She said, "If you've been here, you know. Everybody is about to get three days off, paid. Three days. That's how long before we'll be back."

She said that the NKVD would wave their guns around for a few minutes. Then they would actually dismantle a bit of the equipment and take it back with them to the prison. "In three days, they'll allow me to buy it back. The weekly bribe will go up by about 10 cases. They'll create a bunch of official paperwork about a big new raid, only they'll change the address of the warehouse on the paperwork. The paperwork will please their bosses. We'll be up and running in no time. It's all a fucking game."

Linna looked around and laughed.

"Just the cost of doing business," she said.

"But quicker this time?"

"Yeah," she said. "Not six months. Not close. More like three."

She walked over to meet her NKVD friends. Artur was staring out of the office window, his nose nearly pressed to the glass.

"Do you see him?" I said.

"No."

"Doesn't mean—"

"No shit," he said. "Krutov could be sitting outside in his car."

"Linna said it's earlier than it should be."

"Way fucking earlier. Months earlier. It's never happened before. Like, never close to this."

"Let's not jump to conclusions."

"But—"

"But let's be smart about it," I said. "First things first. Where are the negatives?"

"In the bottom drawer of the last filing cabinet," Artur said. He indicated the cabinet with a flick of his nose. "They're in the envelope, addressed like you said, all ready."

"Good, good. So, let's stick with the plan."

"Meaning?"

"Meaning that we get the fuck away from each other," I said. "You go hide in one of the toilet stalls. And me—"

I looked over at the coat rack in the corner. There was a green cap hanging on one of the hooks. I put it on.

"How's it look?"

"Fine, I guess."

"Just a slight change," I said, and then I thought about it and put the hat back on the hook. "He saw me with a hat and scarf. Better to be bare-headed now. You hide in the shitter, and I'll sit in my van. Anything happens to me, you send the envelope. Anything happens to you, I send the envelope. Got it?"

"I guess so."

"No guesses. It's a simple plan."

Artur walked to the toilet, and I walked back to the van and began faux-fussing with my clipboard. Linna was right: the whole thing was a lark. The guns were put away within about a minute, and everybody was laughing. The head trench coat, whoever he was — definitely not Krutov — talked to Linna, and then he and the rest of the trench coats withdrew. They left the three soldiers behind, and they seemed intent on dismantling one of the distilling machines that I really didn't understand. There was a kettle, and some copper tubing, and I didn't know what else. Anyway, the soldiers took it apart — but only after a couple of my co-workers lent them wrenches and showed them the places where the apparatus could be disassembled into manageable chunks.

Every few minutes, a trench coat would come back inside to check on the progress of the disassembly. Two different trench coats, neither of them Krutov.

At a certain point, one of the trench coats walked over to me. I did everything but shout "oh, fuck" as he walked across the warehouse. A quick peek to my left and right confirmed that there were no vehicles and no people in my immediate vicinity. He was coming for me. Oh, fuck. I actually fingered the pistol in my jacket pocket, the pistol I seemed to be carrying all the time. The idea that I would be able to shoot my way out of there was absurd. I was 200 feet from the warehouse entrance, and the soldiers would be able to drop the wrenches and pick up the rifles before I reached the door. Then again, maybe I could just make a run for it in the van. Then again, who was I kidding? The cavalry was just outside and, even if they were relaxed, the gun shot would certainly awaken them.

Oh, fuck.

"Do I know you?" the trench coat said.

"Don't think so," I said. It definitely wasn't Krutov, but I had no idea if he was a Krutov emissary.

"You sure?"

"Pretty sure."

The trench coat stopped, got a little closer — he was looking at me through the open driver's window — and stared for maybe five seconds. That's a long fucking time to be stared at from three feet away.

"I guess not," the trench coat said. "We're taking the van this time."

"You need this?" I held up the clipboard.

"No, keep your fucking schedules."

I opened the door and said, "Key is in the ignition."

The trench coat started the van and looked at me.

"Anything in the back?"

"Eight cases, I think."

"Our secret, yes," he said.

"What cases?" I said.

"Good man," the trench coat said. He put the van into gear and drove it out of the warehouse, presumably across the parking lot to be stored in the prison lot until Linna bought it back in three days. What a business.

My biggest concern at that instant was whether I had soiled the upholstery. Then, standing there with the clipboard, leaning against a wall, waiting for my heart rate to return to normal, all I could wonder was if it was possible that the whole thing was just a coincidence. Could it not mean anything that, a couple of days after I had blackmailed an NKVD agent into seeking a transfer to the ass end of nowhere, his co-workers were barging in three months early on their extortion timetable? Really, could it just be, I don't know, happenstance?

I hated coincidences. Everybody who worked in my business hated coincidences. But, given everything I could see, that's what it appeared to be. Krutov was nowhere to be seen, and everybody else in the place couldn't have been happier with the outcome of the NKVD field trip. My co-workers actually let out a group cheer when the last of the NKVD soldiers left. He was carrying the lid of the enormous kettle under one arm with his rifle slung over the opposite shoulder.

After I rescued him from and toilet and calmed him down in the office, Artur and I joined the rest for the celebration of an unexpected three-day paid holiday. Coincidence. Just a coincidence. The one thing I did notice at the bar was that it wasn't until our third drink that the tremor in Artur's hand settled down.

38

One more visit to The Rock, and I figured I would qualify for the friends and family discount. Then again, who was I kidding? If that was the case, they would have had to have been paying the guy sleeping on the end of the bar for every drink.

On the drive to Tartu, I actually felt decent about things. For one, I didn't need to arrange more time off from Linna by going into my pathetic-widower act — the NKVD holiday took care of that. But it was more than that. I was pretty sure that Artur's situation was going to work out — not positive but pretty sure — and I felt some satisfaction in that. I also was hopeful about the odious Karl Tamm, too. And if I was a little worried about how to play it if he balked again, I just had a sense that he wasn't going to balk this time. I mean, he had promised the last time — and if you couldn't trust the word of a Jew-killing Nazi wannabe who looked like a cross between a gorilla and a giraffe, well, who could you trust?

The drill was the same as the last time — Leks waited out in the Saab, and Rikkart sat at the table in the main bar. Both were carrying their lady guns. I was in the nook, behind the half-doors, with four beers this time, three for him and one for me.

Tamm was, as always, on time. He also was, as always, thirsty. He downed the first beer and half of the second before his belch announced his intention to speak.

"So, you ready to do this?" he said.

"Yes, absolutely." I actually felt some joy in my heart.

"I've said my goodbyes."

"And how did that go?"

"How do you think it went, asshole?" Tamm said. "It was awful. It was fucking awful. I lived with those men. I fought with those men. They're my brothers. Fuck. How do you think it went?"

I was immediately sorry that I had asked the question, but there was no way to un-ask it. All I could do was sip and listen, listen and sip. Tamm took a few seconds downing the rest of the second beer before continuing.

"We drank every bottle we had," he said. "We stayed up all night — I mean, I know I didn't sleep. A couple of them want to come with me..."

"Wait a minute. There's no fucking way. That's not the deal."

"Easy, asshole," Tamm said. "I told them. I told them about Hansi, how he wanted me. None of them were ever under his command, but some of them are jealous. Some of them are mad. Christ."

Tamm attacked the third beer. I tried to think of a way to wrap this up, so we could get started on the drive. I could just stand up and say, "Ready?" But, well, I didn't want to insult him, and he seemed entirely insult-able in his state. The guy was a walking, talking exposed nerve-ending at that point.

I really wanted him to settle down on his own. And I really wanted it to be quickly. And he did, after the third beer was finished and the second half of mine.

"All right," he said. Again, my heart leapt.

"We just have to go pick up my trunk," he said.

"Your what?"

"My trunk. It's a fucking trunk. You ever heard of it? It's where you store things. We need to go get it."

"And where is it?"

"In the forest," Tamm said.

"No. Fuck no. No fucking way. The forest? No fucking way."

I was half shouting at Tamm, and I didn't regret it. We were both leaning over the table, nearly nose to nose. Only when I really looked at him did I back off — physically, but not verbally.

"We're not going on some holiday cruise," I said. "And we're not going into those woods to get any goddamned trunk."

"Then I'm not going."

"For fuck's sake—"

"Then I'm not going," Tamm said. "My whole life is in that trunk. And if you think that's pathetic, well, fuck you. But it's my whole life, and it takes two men to carry it more than a few yards, and we're going back in there to get it, and then you're taking me to see Hansi."

"Be serious—"

"It's my whole life."

"You're starting a new life."

"Not without the trunk," he said. And then we were just sitting there and looking at each other.

Just then, as he had the previous times, Rikkart arrived at the half-doors with two more beers. I took them and put them both in front of Tamm.

"You fucking wait here," I said, and then I was out through the swinging half-doors. The first thing I said to Rikkart was, "Go get Leks," and then I went over to the bar for a shot to go with my next beer.

39

"No sweat," Leks said, for the third time. "Really, not a problem. Not a problem at all."

The three of us were sitting in the bar. Tamm was in the nook with his two beers. I figured that we had five minutes to figure this out, five minutes tops, before Tamm got antsy and/or the beers were finished.

I liked to think that I was a prepared kind of spy, and that I anticipated most of the potential pitfalls and planned for detours around them. One thing I had never considered was the possibility that Tamm would want to go back into the forest.

When Rikkart looked at my face and said, "Wow, even you didn't see this one coming," I nodded quickly in reply. The kid's face fell. It must have been like the first time — after the initial flush of pride — when a boy found himself able to figure out an arithmetic problem faster than his father, or kick a ball farther — that the old man wasn't all-powerful. Although, it wasn't not exactly the same, seeing as how Rikkart hadn't seen this one coming, either. What did they call it in American baseball?

"Quite a curveball," I said, more a mutter than a statement. Both Leks and Rikkart said, "What?" I waved them off.

"The idea of driving into those fucking woods to potentially run into those fucking Forest Brothers, I don't know," I said. "But I don't think we have a choice."

"Not a problem," Leks said.

"I mean—"

"Not a problem," he said. "I can get us to the clearing from when we drove the last time. It's easy. That has to be where he left the trunk, or at least close to there. We go in, we pick it up, we leave."

"And if the Forest Brothers disagree with your plan?" I said.

"Why would they?" Leks said. "He's their brother. They have their bond. From what you said, they spent the night reminiscing and shit. They're not going to disagree."

"But, well—" Rikkart said. Leks really was the operator of the pair. Rikkart was more of a tourist than a participant. It was probably like he was sitting in the back of a taxi driving wildly through the streets, weaving in and out of traffic. You do that, and it's like you're on a roller-coaster — kind of scared but not really, as if the whole thing isn't quite real.

"Look," I said. "We don't have a choice here. Or, rather, I don't have a choice. You two can bail out now, with the money and with my thanks. You've been great."

The two of them looked at each other.

Rikkart said, "Fuck you, Uncle. We're in."

"Under my rules," I said. "And, really, it's only one rule. If I sense any danger, or if there is any shooting, you guys both go out the driver's side door and into the woods. Got it?" They nodded.

"No bullshit," I said. "You're going to park on the side of the clearing that's closest to the main road, with the driver's side right against the woods. Either on my word, or on the sound of the first shot, you're out the door and into those fucking woods, running your asses off toward the main road. Got it?"

They both nodded.

"Say it," I said.

They both said it.

I looked at my watch. Five minutes were up.

"Showtime," I said.

Tamm had finished the beers and his hands were folded in front of him on the table. I didn't sit down. I just said, "Let's go," and we did. The four of us walked out to the Saab like four buddies heading out for a country drive — well, three buddies and a giraffe. Leks drove and Rikkart sat next to him. I sat in the back next to Tamm. The pistol and the handcuffs were still in my jacket pockets.

Leks looked over his shoulder.

"The same clearing where they bring the girls?" he said, and Tamm nodded.

I was shocked how short a drive it was — bumpy and slow on the narrow dirt track, yes, but not far at all into the woods. The idea that the Forest Brothers were that close to civilization, and the Soviet army, and still managed to stay hidden — well, the last bunch of them, anyway — was a testament to something, although I wasn't sure what. It was either the cunning of the Forest Brothers or the ineptitude of the army. It was probably a bit of both.

It was only a couple of minutes before the clearing presented itself. Leks did as he was told, entering the large square area and maneuvering the car to the left. He parked as instructed, with his door abutting the side of the woods nearest to the main road, nearest to Tartu proper.

"Okay, where's the trunk?" I said.

"Just over there," Tamm said, pointing straight ahead. "In the woods there, maybe 10 feet deep."

"You two stay here," I said, and Rikkart and Leks nodded. "We'll go get it and then we'll be out of here."

I opened the door on the forest side, and Tamm opened the door on the clearing side. I was first, and had a foot out the door, when his door opened. That's when the shot rang out, shattering the glass.

"You all right?" I yelled.

"Fine. Fine."

"Not hit?"

"Don't think so," Tamm said. "No, not hit."

"You two, get the fuck out of here — now."

Leks and Rikkart didn't need to be told twice. They were out the driver's side and into the woods in about five seconds. No more shots were fired. The Saab must have been between the shooter and their escape route.

"You have a gun?" I said.

Tamm shook his head. "In the trunk," he said.

"Perfect."

"I only have a knife."

"For cutting your own throat? Jesus."

I was having trouble catching my breath. Tamm was impatient. It wasn't 10 seconds of thinking and trying to calm down, but Tamm blurted out, "So, what do we do?"

"Not sure. Let me think."

"We're sitting ducks here."

"But we're protected by the car, too," I said. "Just give me a second to think. Just fucking relax."

"Asshole."

"You sit there or I'll shoot you, or I'll push you out of the car and let them shoot you," I said. "And, in the meantime, you should probably try to figure out which one of your Forest Fucking Brothers is a forest fucking rat."

40

Other than the single shot that shattered the window on Tamm's door, there had been no other shooting. We were scrunched down as low as we could be in the back of the car. Our heads were barely below window level.

"I think we drive it out of here and pray," I said.

"Why not the woods where those kids went?"

"Because we're not kids. I'm really not a kid. All in all—"

That was when the second shot came. It hit the car on the passenger side.

"Look, I'm going to snake into the front seat — out my door, into the front door. Here's my pistol. When I get it started, I'll gun it and then—"

"I gun it," Tamm said.

I got out and then in without another shot being fired. But when I half sat up and turned the key, a blast of bullets was fired into the front of the car. It was as if they weren't aiming for me, not directly. They wanted to disable the car by blowing a hole in the radiator, if nothing else, and they succeeded. The engine sputtered and died in the silence.

"The woods, then?" Tamm said.

"The woods."

But as I opened the door, there was another blast. This one was unmistakable, from a machine gun. The direction was unmistakable, too, from the side of the woods nearest to Tartu. God, if those kids had gotten caught.

"They've moved," I said.

"No shit."

"And which one of your buddies has a machine gun? And why the fuck are they shooting at us?"

"I don't know," Tamm said, softly but loudly enough to be heard in the interval between machine gun blasts.

I tried the driver's side door again and was greeted by another rat-a-tat from the machine gun. I tried the passenger side door and was met by a different kind of fire — rifles probably, and more than one.

That we were trapped went without saying. Then into the quiet, into the clearing in the woods that now smelled of cordite and human fear, a voice shouted.

"Come out with your hands up and the shooting stops," it said.

I looked at Tamm.

"You recognize the voice?"

"No?"

"Do you think you would recognize the voice?"

"Yes," he said. "Maybe. I mean, I've lived my life with them. They're my brothers, my goddamned brothers."

I was able to peek over the back seat, back at Tamm, and his face showed a man who was stunned. Amid all of the commotion, he felt enough to shed a single tear, which he flicked away with his finger.

"Look, we don't have a choice here," I said.

Tamm said nothing.

"If they're really your friends, it's our best option."

Again, nothing from Tamm.

"Fucking face it. They have rifles. They have a machine gun. They only fire when we make a move. If they'd wanted to kill us, they could have done it by now. Instead, they make the offer. If they're your friends"

"They're my brothers," Tamm said.

"Then give me back the pistol, and let's go meet your fucking brothers," I said.

He handed me the gun. I opened my door first, and there was no new blast of gunfire. I got out of the car and raised my hands over my head. Maybe five seconds later, Tamm opened his door and did the same. Again, there was no gunfire.

"Walk away from the car into the middle of the clearing," came the disembodied voice from within the woods. We did as we were told, ending up in the middle of the clearing, maybe 30 feet from the tree line in every direction.

We stood there and waited for probably 20 seconds before the voice emerged from the woods, along with a half-dozen others. The half-dozen were dressed as soldiers. The voice was dressed in a black trench coat.

"What the?" Tamm said.

"The NKVD is what the," I said.

"But—"

"Like I said: one of your Forest Fucking Brothers is a forest fucking rat."

"But it can't—"

"It can and it is," I said.

Slowly, the trench coat and his minions advanced toward where Tamm and I were standing. Like, really slowly — step, pause, pause again, step. There was enough time for me to give myself absolution — there was no way to have seen this coming — but not enough time to figure a way out.

Step, pause, pause, step.

Step, pause, pause, step.

All of their eyes were on us. Mine wandered a little, searching for I-didn't-know what. Over the shoulder of the farthest soldier on the left, maybe 50 feet behind him, I noticed a flicker of movement in the trees. Then more than a flicker. Rikkart and Leks were standing there, lady guns in hand.

I did my best to lock eyes with Rikkart. It wasn't easy from that distance, maybe 80 feet, maybe 100. I did my best, and a shook my head as insistently as I dared.

Rikkart and Leks didn't move.

I shook my ahead again.

This time, Rikkart advanced a step.

I stared him down as hard as I could, and then I shook my head a third time, and then I stared some more. I still couldn't tell if our eyes had met.

Rikkart began to take another step in our direction. I didn't know what else to do. A shout made no sense, accomplishing nothing. A pistol shot made no sense, either. It would just get us dead.

So, I stared. I looked as hard as I could, burning a hole through Rikkart with my eyes, and I held my breath. One. Two. And then I saw Leks grab him from behind, clamping his hand over his left shoulder.

At that moment, the look on Rikkart's face changed from something that originally had been a kind of defiant fright into something softer, sadder. I continued to stare as Leks kept his hand on Rikkart's shoulder and then turned him. And then, after a quick pause, the two of them began running back into the woods, back toward Tartu.

PART IV

41

The cells were in the basement, of course. There was a bucket in the corner, of course. They took our clothes, of course. Pre-war or post-war, Gestapo or NKVD, Cologne or Lyon or Budapest or Estonia, it was as if they were all working out of the same instruction manual.

They blindfolded us in the truck. We drove for about a half-hour from Tartu by my guess, a half-hour give-or-take. We weren't all the way back to Tallinn, not nearly. Somewhere in the middle, then, but that was all I had.

There were two wooden bunks in a cell that was maybe 15 feet by 20. It was cold enough as I lay there that I was shivering. Tamm was much more comfortable, it seemed, if not asleep then reasonably close. Then again, he should be more comfortable given that he'd had the experience of living in the woods for years without heat. Also, he really had the full gorilla-fucks-a-giraffe thing going. He was the hairiest human I had ever seen — and, admittedly, I was using the term "human" loosely. Cutting off his hair would have been like shearing a sheep.

I hugged myself to stay warm and tried to figure out what had happened and what might happen next. It seemed obvious enough, even if Tamm had refused to acknowledge it. The person responsible had to know that Tamm was planning on coming back for the trunk. The only people who knew that were the Forest Brothers who had spent the night drinking and reminiscing and ruing Tamm's decision to leave the forest and rejoin his Nazi mentor. The rat's motive for contacting the NKVD was irrelevant. It was enough to know that there was a rat, and that he was responsible.

I sat up at one point, and Tamm pointed at me.

"There is this one guy," he said. As he continued on, his voice rose from a whisper at the start to something louder, more emphatic.

"I'm wracking my brain, and I keep coming back to the same guy. Really, I keep coming back to one thing he said last night. We were all pretty drunk — we wiped out every bottle we had. And it was late, late enough that it was almost early, and there were four of us who hadn't passed out. We were sitting around the embers of the fire, and this guy, he said, 'You ever wonder how we made it this long, after so many of the other got caught or just quit?'

"And I said, 'We made it because we're the fucking best,' and the other guys all raised their bottles and repeated 'the fucking best.' Except this guy, he kept going. This guy, he said, 'Sometimes I wonder if they like having a few of us out here — you know, so that they have a reason to be here, too. So that the Soviet army in Estonia has something to do.'"

Tamm stopped talking. I grabbed myself in a shiver.

"Doesn't make him a rat, I don't think," I said.

"I do."

"He just sounds like a philosopher of sorts, not a rat."

"He sounds like a rat."

"Whatever," I said. "But, then again, it really doesn't matter.

We're in here, and that's that. It really doesn't matter who put us here."

"It fucking matters to me," Tamm said, quietly. And then he closed his eyes again.

All through the night, the cells had been quiet. I had not heard a sound from any of the others. Then again, I was only assuming that there were others because, in my experience, there had always been others. But we had been blindfolded until we were inside, so I didn't really know.

Still, it had been quiet. If anyone was being tortured, it wasn't within earshot. I closed my eyes and easily imagined, too easily, all manner of contraptions that might be used to encourage a suspect to dispense some vital information. I thought about the loppers for removing fingers and toes and the pliers for pulling out finger-nails. There were always rubber hoses, too — and, in Lyon, there had been hot and cold baths. In the end, though, I always got back to the electric clips that would be attached on one end to a battery and on the other end to my balls. It was the nightmare I had never been able to shake, even if it had never happened to me. But I had seen the metal clips before in the jails in Cologne and Lyon, the clips and the battery. And I looked down and noticed my hands had moved, more involuntarily than voluntarily, to shield my balls.

I ran my hand along the surface of the bunk. It was varnished — a luxury, in my jail cell experience. It meant I wasn't likely to catch a splinter in my bare ass. I thought about that, and then I half laughed. It was amazing what ran through your mind when you were trying to avoid thinking about reality. In my case — our case, mine and Tamm's — the reality was that we were fucked. As in dead. And what then? The asshole Gerhard Grimm wouldn't lift a finger, but Fritz Ritter would. He would try to find out what happened, as best as he could. But in Estonia? Under the Soviets? In the end, there would be no information to be found and no retribution to be had. They might as well plant a sapling over my grave.

A noise startled me and woke Tamm from his semi-slumber. It was the jangle of keys in the door, followed by the squeal of rusty hinges. A soldier tossed our clothes into the middle of the room and said, "Five minutes." Then, one more noise: a slam.

42

There were no blindfolds this time, just two guys with two rifles. They directed us out of the cells and up a staircase. I took another peek at my watch, which had somehow survived the crash and then a bounce on the concrete floor of the cell when the soldier tossed in our clothes. It was almost noon. We had been in custody for roughly 20 hours.

When we reached the main floor, what appeared to be the front door was open to our left. The soldiers directed us in the other direction, though, pointing with the rifles. In the back, I assumed, was where the interrogations took place.

But we walked past office door after office door, all closed. We got to the end, and there was only a single door in front of us, heavier than the office doors and without a window.

"Keep going," one of the soldiers said.

I opened the door, and we walked down three steps and into a parking area of some sort. It was paved. The sun was bright, and it took a few seconds for my eyes to adjust. I took a quick look around and wondered if I could make a run for it. I could see that Tamm was doing the same thing, making the same calculation. The smart thing would be for us to work together on something, but who the hell was I kidding? It was all for one and fuck the other guy at that point.

But there were too many other soldiers in the parking area, too many other rifles. And then, taking one more scan, I saw the van — white, nondescript, parked over on the far right. The back was open, and I squinted when I looked inside, and I saw cases of something stacked inside, cases of...

And then I saw the driver's side door open up and Linna get out.

What?

I thought of a dozen things in the next three seconds, none of which either registered or made sense.

And then one of the rifles said, "Unload."

Tamm and I approached the van.

Linna smiled when our eyes met.

"What the—" I said.

"Captain says to unload first, talk later," the rifle said.

Tamm and I each grabbed a case and headed in the direction where the rifle was pointing. The cases held 12 bottles apiece, and I always found them to be heavy when carried any real distance. Tamm seemed more comfortable with the load. In those few seconds, all he had offered me was a crooked eyebrow.

We marched the cases back inside the building and up some stairs, two flights, two soldiers behind us, to what was clearly an interrogation/torture room that had been commandeered for a more important purpose. I couldn't help but look around. There were loppers hanging on a peg in the wall, but I didn't see any metal clips or batteries. Still, my balls involuntarily shriveled.

Linna? What the hell? Pretty quickly, my mind was clearing of the fuzz and the fear. The adrenaline was flowing again. How had she found us, and what was the play? It didn't seem possible that she was trading us for a van-load of vodka. All I knew, based on the soldier's words, is that we would be speaking after the vodka had been delivered.

There were 10 cases overall, five times up the stairs, five times down. But the third trip, the fatter soldier was winded enough that he waved the other one up as a solo escort while he leaned on the van and waited with Linna.

Coming back down the stairs, the guard behind us, Tamm looked at me with a question on his face. I got it: was now the time to make a move, to take a chance on overtaking the single guard? That would have to be a two-man maneuver, and I shook my head. Tamm stared even more insistently at me, and I tried to match his intensity and shook my head again. I mean, even if we did manage to take down the guard on the stairs and get his rifle that would have left us outgunned by about a factor of eight.

By the fourth trip, Linna had managed to sidle her way around to the back of the van and say to me, "When the time comes, get in the driver's seat." I nodded and half smiled. At least she had thought of something.

After the fifth trip up and down, we came out of the building. Again, it took a second for my eyes to adjust to the brightness. The fatter guard grimaced as he raised himself from the bumper, then walked toward us and announced to all, "The boss says you have five minutes. No more."

The unloading complete, most of our security detail went inside the building. The fatter soldier and his partner positioned themselves about 30 feet away, and leaned on their rifles, and laughed about something — likely, what they might be doing with the 10 cases now stacked in the torture room. I did hear the partner say, "This is the most interesting day we've had in weeks — and there's enough up there for 10 parties after we're done."

I had to admit, I didn't like the sound of the word "done." I couldn't help thinking that it was a euphemism for something else.

Tamm and I walked over to Linna. I kicked the van's right front tire and said, "Already bought it back from your buddies at the prison, I see."

"Among other things," Linna said.

Then she said, "Let's walk away from the van a little. Makes it seem less, I don't know. Just more natural. Less suspicious. I don't know."

But she was wrong.

"Stay with the van," the fatter soldier said, pointing again with the rifle. Then he went back to laughing with his partner.

43

"So, what is this five minutes?" I said. "What do you have up your sleeve?"

Tamm watched, listened. He wouldn't say anything, not a word, during the whole time. He was an observer, and clearly baffled besides. Then again, it would have been unusual for a cross between a gorilla and a giraffe to possess a poker face.

"You don't think 10 cases buy the freedom of the great Forest Brother, do you?" Linna said. "Or, for that matter, the freedom of Alex Kovacs, the great German spy."

I stared her down, hard. I was about to say something, to ask her, and half formed the word "how" before she stopped me.

"How do I know? How did I find out? I've known since you were taking pictures at the rail yard in the middle of the night. It wasn't hard. You were too comfortable, too smug."

"But—"

"It doesn't fucking matter," she said. "We have five minutes. The vodka bought us a conversation, nothing more. Five minutes."

"But I'm not actually—"

This time, Linna touched her index finger to my lips. It was a gesture that was insistent on the one hand but oddly tender on the other.

"Later," she said. "Later for the history lesson."

She went on to explain in about three sentences that she was tipped off to our arrests by her NKVD contact at the prison. I assumed it was the officer she seemed so creepily comfortable with, although I guess it didn't really matter who told her.

"Try to look like you're not about to shit yourselves," Linna said. "All these two know is that their captain told them to let us talk for five minutes. They probably figure there's another shoe to drop, and that you're going to get released, and that the captain is going to get greased. Doesn't matter, though, because they're not going to let you go. There isn't enough grease in Estonia to spring a Forest Brother and a German spy. The publicity value is just too great. As my contact at the prison said, 'No chance. Those newspaper clippings will likely get sent to Stalin himself.' But he did get me the five minutes."

"Wasn't that a huge risk?" I said. "I mean—"

"Not that huge," she said. "We have a business relationship that he wants to continue. Two relationships — the vodka and, well..."

Linna stopped. My face must have betrayed something, but I don't know what it was. Maybe it was disgust at the thought of sleeping with the NKVD in order to run the bootleg vodka business. Maybe it was me somehow feeling a measure of hurt or jealousy. I didn't think that was possible, though. At least in my head, I didn't think it was possible.

Anyway, she shook her head and said, "Just business." Then a little quieter, "Just business."

Linna looked at her watch.

"They think we'll take the full five minutes. They will relax a little bit over the time, and then be more mindful as we get toward five minutes. So, at three minutes, that's when we'll make our move."

"Our move?"

At this, Linna turned so that her back was to the two guards and said, "I have a pistol." Except that she mouthed the words more than she said them.

"They searched the van but not me," she said. "Well, not completely. The patted down my jacket and reached into the pocket. They didn't check, you know, there."

She looked down at her crotch, just a quick glance.

I was doing the mental calculation — lady gun at 30 feet — and didn't love the odds. She read my mind and said, "It's bigger than you think. See how loose the jumper is? It hides a lot."

The jumper did, in fact, hang to the top of her thighs.

"It's big enough, and I can handle it," she said.

Linna looked at her watch.

"Thirty seconds," she said.

I counted down in my head. At 10 seconds, she said, "All right, Forest Brother, walk behind me and put your feet up on the step below the van door and pretend to tie the lace of your boot."

Tamm did as he was told, and Linna kind of eased over nearer the truck so that he was blocking the view of the guards, at least a little. She reached into her waistband and pulled out the pistol, and it was a decent size. She would have a chance.

"Let me," I said, in a half-whisper.

"Fuck you, my Alex," she said.

Then it was all noise and cordite. Bang, bang — two shots, both hits. Before the second guard had fallen, the skinnier one, I had leaped into the driver's seat as Linna had instructed. She and Tamm jumped into the passenger seat, but not before she admired her handiwork for a full beat. The three of us were three-across in the front seat because there was no back seat. We were three-across, Linna in the middle, and barreling out of the parking lot in the direction of I-didn't-know-where.

"Where did you learn to shoot like that?" I said.

Linna turned her heard toward me, and I saw her lips start to move, to purse. It was a vision I carried for a long time thereafter. But, before she could answer my question, a single rifle shot rang out from behind us. The van doors had not been secured before we sped off, and they were flapping open and shut as we accelerated.

One shot.

Linna's head exploded all over the cab of the van, speckling Tamm and me with blood and meaty bits. I heard myself scream, and then I felt myself wiping something the size of a lingonberry off of my face. And then, in the rear-view mirror, I saw the guard — the fatter guard — sitting up and firing a second shot. It missed.

44

I didn't know what I was thinking. I didn't know where I was going. I just drove as fast as I could and tried not to fixate on the fact that Linna's dead hand had splayed onto my right thigh.

After two or three minutes, we came to a bigger road and to a sign that said "Tallinn" with an arrow pointing to the left. I was about to make the turn to the left when Tamm said, "We need to dump her."

Christ.

"We're not dumping her," I said.

"If the cops stop us, or worse—"

"Will you look at this?" I said. I waved at the blood-spattered windscreen, and the blood-spattered instrument panel, and then at the puddle on the floor of the cab.

"Look at that, look at yourself," I said, and Tamm did. He, like I, was painted with blood and brain matter. He picked a piece off of his trousers and flicked it onto the floor.

"If the NKVD stops us, if a fucking traffic cop stops us, we're not going to be able to talk ourselves out of this, this mess — body or no body. So, we're not fucking dumping her."

I made the left turn. Tamm lifted Linna's body, and more blood gushed out of her head. He lifted her over the back of the seat and laid her in the cargo area of the van. Then he found a rag in the glove box and wiped up the seat. The blood had begun to seep into the upholstery, and the rag absorbed most of the rest.

"So, where?"

"Tallinn," I said.

"Still to Hansi, then?"

"Still to Hansi."

I wanted to cry but I couldn't. Grief was not a luxury I could afford. I stomped on the accelerator and stared through the red speckles on the windscreen and tried to think of my next move. I guessed that following the original plan made the most sense. I would take Tamm to Antti's boat, and travel with him to Suomenlinna, and be done with it.

Suomenlinna. Christ. I asked Antti once, in the middle of one our voyages, and he said that Linna meant "like a castle, or a fortress. So Suomenlinna means, like, fortress of Finland." Christ.

I kept repeating to myself as I drove — and I didn't know how long I had been driving — that I had nothing to do with her death, that it had all been her decision to get involved. And while that was true, well, the reason she made the decision was because of me. Because she felt something for me — a kinship, a friendship, maybe more. Because she felt something for me, and because I had allowed her to feel something for me.

And then two phrases competed in my head for attention.

One, a gruff male voice:

"Only whores, Alex. Only whores."

The second, a female:

"Fuck you, my Alex."

At a certain point, I did sob, just for a second. I didn't think

Tamm noticed. It might have lasted longer, except for the flashing blue and white lights ahead of us that had suddenly seized my attention.

"Oh, shit," Tamm said.

"Yeah," I said.

"Do you see a turnoff?"

"No, do you?"

There were two police vehicles forming an impromptu road block about a quarter-mile ahead. It was a straight road in the middle of nowhere, farm fields on either side. There were four officers — just regular cops, it appeared — standing on the pavement. One of them accompanied the blue and white flashing lights with a large red flag that he waved back and forth over his head.

Tamm looked into the back of the van, past Linna's body.

"There's no vodka," he said.

"No, no vodka. But it doesn't really matter. A bribe wasn't going to work."

"But they're just local cops, and you know—"

"It wouldn't work," I said. "Not with those two soldiers Linna shot back in that courtyard. No, there's no bribe for that."

"We still have her pistol," Tamm said. He had been holding it the whole time we were driving.

"Not enough. There's four of them, and I'm sure they're all armed, and maybe with more than pistols. One isn't enough. Four against one — the math doesn't add up to anything but a massacre."

I had reduced my speed by half as we approached the road-block. We were still about 1,000 feet away. We were going to have to slow down by half again if the cops weren't to be alarmed, so that's what I did.

"So, what?" Tamm said.

I didn't answer.

Five hundred feet.

"So?"

I didn't answer.

Three hundred feet.

Two hundred feet.

One hundred feet.

We were almost into a rolling stop when I shouted, "Hang on."

I floored the accelerator, and the cops didn't have the time to grab their weapons, to do anything but dive out of the way. I saw the red flag fly into the air as I crashed between the two police cars. It was, as it turned out, a really half-assed roadblock, with the cars nose-to-nose and not overlapping. At my speed, they peeled apart easily.

I heard two shots come from behind as we sped off. One of them hit the back door of the van, but that was it. About two minutes ahead, there was a turnoff onto a bigger road that said, "Tallinn center 20 km." We were back into the outskirts of the city in maybe 15 minutes, and I got off the road at the first sign of something familiar. It would be city streets after that.

"Where to now?" Tamm said. He was still fingering Linna's pistol.

"One stop, and then the boat to Helsinki," I said.

45

Looking back on it, the whole idea of going back to the warehouse was an idiotic risk. I had to do it, though. The more I thought about it, it was the only way. There would be too many innocent people affected otherwise, too many people and too much collateral damage. It was the only way.

I parked the van right behind the warehouse. We rolled up the windows, and locked it, and hoped that nobody got too nosy. Before I got out, I looked back one last time at Linna. The way her body was arranged, you couldn't see the hole in the back of her head.

We went into the back door of the warehouse. It being Saturday, I expected to see exactly one employee and, from the distance, I could see the light was on in Artur's office. Saturday was his day for balancing the ledgers. Always Saturday.

"Toilet's over there," I said, and then I pointed. Tamm nodded.

"Vodka's over there — help yourself." I pointed again, this time to the part of the warehouse where the bottling was completed and the vodka bottles were waiting to be put into the cases.

"Just don't make any noise, and don't make yourself conspicuous," I said. "And if the NKVD comes in — anybody wearing a uniform or a black trench coat — use your best judgment. But if it was me, I'd just start unloading the pistol on them. Oh, and praying."

Tamm looked back and forth, unsure of his first move. Ultimately, he decided to grab a bottle and take it with him to the toilet. I walked over to Artur's office and knocked lightly on the door jamb, but I still startled him. And after he got a look at me, startled morphed into horrified.

"My God," he said. "Have you seen yourself? What happened?"

I took a quick look down at my shirt, my sleeves, my hands, and they were all still blood-stained. Then I threw myself into the chair across from his desk and told Artur that Linna was dead. And if I couldn't remember the last time I had seen someone's face go white, I would never forget how Artur's did when I told him that her body was parked in the van. I'll never forget his face, or how his hands began to shake.

He pulled a bottle out of his desk drawer and poured a measure for both of us, somehow managing not to spill any. We finished that one, and he poured another, and then he made the toast, "To Linna. My boss. My friend."

He asked for details, and I told him everything, beginning at the beginning. I told him that I was an agent, and that I had been given an assignment to get one of the Forest Brothers out of the country, and Artur's mouth fell open and stayed open, just a little. He had known I had a hidden life, or guessed, but I wasn't sure even he imagined the reality.

I kept talking, and it looked like he was breathing through his mouth exclusively. When I got to the part about Linna coming to our rescue, I sketched in what I could based upon what she had told us. That is, I told him that she had gotten the information from the NKVD creep across the way, and that her bribe had bought us nothing more than a conversation, and that she shot the two guards after that conversation, and then...

Artur closed his mouth when I was done, and he put his hand over it, and his head kind of fell forward, and his eyes closed. Four. Five. Six. Seven. Then his eyes were open again, open and sad.

"Well, we're fucking done, out of business," he said. "I feel like a shithead even thinking about it, but I kind of feel like it's my responsibility now that she's gone. All of the men who work here, my responsibility. But if she used that asshole over at the prison, and then she shot those guards with his information and maybe killed them — all the bribes, all the relationships, they won't be able to overcome that. We're done. Finished. Christ."

He had been leaning over the desk, but now he kind of fell backward into his chair, eyes now focused on the ceiling.

"There might be a way," I said. "It's why I came back."

He looked at me, staring through narrow slits.

"How?"

"You turn us in," I said, and Artur didn't get it.

"You call the fellas across the parking lot and tell them you found the van, that you found Linna. Then you say you came into the warehouse, to use your office phone to call them, and that you spotted me and Tamm. You say that we were covered in blood, and that we panicked when you saw us, and that we ran into the toilet and locked the door. And we'll leave the pistol behind, over by the vodka. We'll make sure it's empty."

"But why?"

"It's Linna's gun," I said. "It's the murder weapon. And we left it, I guess, because we were out of bullets."

After that, I told him what I thought would happen. It was

just a guess, but a decent one, a realistic one. I figured that the cavalry would run across the parking lot, and they'd find Linna, and they'd find the murder weapon, and they'd break down the toilet door and find nothing but an open window with blood stains on the sash.

"And, what does that accomplish?" Artur said.

"Not sure," I said. "But it will give them some options, depending on how they want to play it. The more I think about it, Linna's NKVD pal from the prison and the captain he bribed on the other end both have a lot of motivation to make this whole thing disappear. I mean, neither of them looks very good in this, right? So, maybe it all never happened. And maybe this is just a business dispute between co-workers that went horribly wrong, and I killed Linna and left her in the van."

"And what about the other one — what did you call him? Tamm?"

"Come to think of it, you never saw Karl Tamm," I said. "You just saw me. And, come to think of it, you might feed the NKVD a little morsel about Linna and me not getting along. Like, on Thursday, we had some kind of big blowup. You weren't close enough to hear the words, but you heard the yelling."

Artur thought about it and said, "I don't know."

"I don't know either, not for sure. If it's a bit of a long shot, well, the way things stand, you currently have no shot."

Artur thought some more, and made a little bit of a face that I couldn't decipher, and then he said, "And what happens to you?"

And I said, "Into the wind, my friend. It's where I live most of the time, in the wind."

46

W e had to go back to my place for the radio. I got it, and packed a small knapsack, and left the rest of my belongings behind. It wasn't as if I had brought anything of sentimental value from Vienna, mostly because I wasn't sure I owned anything of sentimental value.

We walked along back streets to the cove and waited there for Antti. Tamm was full of questions about what was next. I had no patience for the questions or for him. After my third grunted reply, he exploded.

"I mean, fuck you, asshole," he said.

"I should just fucking shoot you right here."

"Yeah, with what?"

I patted the knapsack. My spare was a borderline lady gun, but it would work from three feet away.

Antti was on time and businesslike toward Tamm. He got us on board, handed us two coffees, and went about the task of piloting the boat to Suomenlinna.

Tamm was suddenly elated, done with the nervous questions. The only thing he asked — and he sounded like a kid wondering when they were going to get to the carnival — was, "And Hansi will be there? Hansi Brugmann will be there?"

"I don't know," I said. I mean, what was I supposed to say, that his Nazi fantasy leader was dead?

"What do you mean, you don't know?"

"What part of 'I don't know' don't you understand? I don't fucking know if he's going to be on the fucking island when we fucking get there. But if he isn't, I'm sure you'll see him soon enough. I'm sure you'll be sucking his Nazi dick in short order."

At that, Tamm stood and balled up his fists. Before, I had at least hinted that I was on his side. More than hinted. Now, I didn't give a shit.

"Sit down, freak," I said. Tamm towered over me. But after a few seconds of staring me down, and then watching me put my hand into the pocket where my pistol now resided, and then taking a peek at Antti, he did sit down.

After we were on the water for about 45 minutes, I hooked up the radio to the boat's battery and typed out my message:

"Cargo arrives at midnight, usual place."

Four minutes later came the reply:

"Message received. Will be there for pickup."

47

Tamm eventually closed his eyes and lay back against the bulkhead, and so did I. The exhaustion was coming at me in waves. It was always like this when I was in the middle of something, but it was worse now. The first guy who said that age was a bitch should be on a postage stamp or a piece of paper currency, not some politician or philosopher.

I needed to sleep but I couldn't sleep, not yet. Soon, but not yet. My body would not allow me to descend into that deepest, most luxurious slumber. Instead, I seemed to drop no further than to the level of surface fog — relaxed but not really. It was sleep, I guessed, but not the restorative kind. I felt no better when I woke up, only, well, foggier.

When this was over, I would descend into something resembling a coma, sleeping 16 hours at a clip for days, maybe a week. It was the sign of the adrenaline ebbing and of my body surrendering. What I felt during that week was less than memorable because I didn't really do much thinking, other than about my next meal and my next nap.

It was the week after the coma that I hated because that was the week when I reflected on what had just happened. Every bad decision, every shitty action, every sliver of valor — they all filled my head. It went without saying that the shitty parts outweighed the valor, at least in my remembering. It tended to take all of my now-restored mental energies to remind myself that the ultimate reality was that I was doing good things for the right reasons.

In the fog, though, in the fog on Antti's boat, with the grotesque Karl Tamm dozing beside me, I had already outlined the parameters of the upcoming debate I would have with myself.

On the one hand, I was delivering this fucking Nazi, this Jew-killer, to some sort of rough justice. I mean, I had no idea what they had planned for Tamm when we got to Suomenlinna, but I knew it was going to be something short of freedom. And even if he was disappearing for a political reason, to avoid a Soviet propaganda bonanza about the massacre of those Jews in Estonia, it was still righteous. There was still, well, that rough justice.

Then there was Artur. What I did in blackmailing Krutov was clearly a noble act. No questions, no indecision, none — and closing down that house, and seeing those three kids, wrapped in towels, being brought out by the lady cops, was a benefit that would take away at least some of the sting. I'd never forget the dead eyes, but still.

I knew, after the coma, I would hang on to those things as tightly as I could within the maelstrom. But it was a maelstrom, and the other memories that rushed by would pry the good thoughts away from me at times, leaving me adrift until I reclaimed them.

The one picture, of me standing there and pissing on a puddle of vodka that had pooled next to the bodies of those two dead NKVD soldiers, dead over a bunch of fucking duty rosters.

The one picture, and the one sound:

"Fuck you, my Alex."

I looked at my watch. I had been in the fog for about a half-hour. I felt as if I had heard Linna's voice in my head, saying the last thing she said to me, six or seven times. Six or seven times in the fog.

"Probably another 20 minutes," Antti said. He pointed, and we could see the few night lights in Helsinki glowing in the distance.

48

Once more to Suomenlinna. Once more around the back side of the little island, the side away from Helsinki, I tried to convince Antti to dock the boat at the King's Gate rather than have me use the dinghy. Once more, Antti told me that I was an idiot, and that King's Gate would be taking an idiotic chance.

"Especially with your grotesque Nazi there," he said.

Antti had inflated the dinghy and was killing some time by working on patching the spare. Tamm was in his own fog, although it seemed to me that he was actually sleeping. It was a bright enough night, enough moon to keep from tripping over the small rocks that protruded from the sandy area where we would land the dinghy.

"Let's go, Tamm," I said, nudging his shoulder with the bottom of my boot. He was startled but focused quickly. At our usual cove, Antti cut the engine and eased to a stop. Then he threw the dinghy into the water and the rope ladder over the side.

Tamm and I bumped, shoulder to shoulder.

"Me first, asshole," I said.

I managed to get down the ladder and into the dinghy without getting wet, a first. The triumph was short-lived, though, seeing as how Tamm nearly capsized the goddamn thing when he got in. As I rowed, we were oriented in a way that I was in the back and he was in the front, leaning forward in clear anticipation. I looked at him and I laughed, and then he looked back at me, and I just waved my hand like it was nothing. Because it was nothing, nothing but the picture in my head of him leaning forward with that ridiculous neck. We looked like the front of one of those Viking ships you saw drawn in the history books.

I beached the dinghy in pretty good order. I mean, I wasn't completely soaked. On the beach, Tamm said, "Now what?"

"Just follow me."

"Is it far?"

"Not far."

As we approached the meeting place, I could see two men waiting. I could only see them in silhouette, though. It made sense, two of them. The idea that Grimm would take Tamm back to Helsinki alone would have been careless — needlessly so. A second man seemed to be the minimum necessary precaution.

At about 100 feet, I recognized Grimm. He and the other man were standing with their hands shoved into their pockets against the chill of the night.

At about 50 feet, Tamm began walking quicker. He was ahead of me now, pulling away.

At 20 feet, he was walking quicker still. He was almost running.

At the end, Tamm bypassed Grimm and headed directly for the other man. He was met by outstretched arms, and then a long embrace.

And then Tamm said. "Brugmann, my God, it's really you."

It took me a second, but only a second. I was standing about

10 feet from Gerhard Fucking Grimm, and I'm pretty sure that my mouth was open. I was standing there, dead in my tracks, staring at Tamm and Hansi Brugmann hugging for a second time. Mouth open, I was trying to process it. Again, it only took a second.

"You lying Nazi mother—"

"Easy, Kovacs. Calm down."

It was Grimm talking. I could see the moon lighting up his teeth. They were very white, whiter than most people's. I had never noticed it before. Grimm was smiling.

"Your mission is complete," he said. "Your best work so far, Alex Kovacs. Really, your best. Bravo. Now, just turn the fuck around and get back on your goddamned boat."

It all hit me. It almost knocked me on my ass. The lie was really the truth. Hansi Brugmann had not died in a German prison after all. He was there, there on the beach, hugging his old Jew-murdering comrade. Why they wanted Tamm, I still wasn't sure. But they wanted him and they got him — thanks to me. I had been used. I had been set up from start to finish. Grimm was a Nazi, Brugmann was a Nazi, Tamm was a Nazi, and I might well just have been standing there on that island with my dick in my hand.

Somewhere, in the whir of thoughts, there also was this question: Had Fritz Ritter been in on the ruse from the beginning or had he been set up, too?

Whirring. I was pretty sure my mouth was still open. I undoubtedly looked stunned because I was stunned. I tried to say something, I didn't know what, but Grimm stopped me.

"Grow up," he said.

49

I could have done what Grimm said. I could have turned around, and gotten back to Antti's boat, and just kept going. Maybe, I should have.

"Humor me," I said.

Grimm paused, not answering. I guess he was trying to decide. I took a quick look over at Brugmann and Tamm. They were no longer hugging. They were standing, side by side, maybe 10 feet from Grimm, listening.

Grimm said, "Okay, what?"

"Why?" I said.

"Why what?"

"Why do you want this fucking animal?" I said. Tamm took a step toward me but Brugmann restrained him with a light touch on his Tamm's arm.

"This fucking animal, as you call him, is an elite military weapon," Grimm said. "Tamm here, he took care of that whole operation — from digging the hole, to supplying the weapons, to getting the vodka that his men needed to get through it, to planting the saplings. Brugmann planned it and directed it, but Tamm, he did it all, including his share of the actual, you know."

I didn't know what to say, and Grimm filled the silence.

"This is a fight that will continue, whether you and your people want it to or not," Grimm said. "You can't control it. The movement is bigger than you'll ever be — underground for now, yes; quiet for now, yes — but bigger, much bigger. And it is men like these two who will help to lead it."

I looked over at Tamm again. He seemed to be standing just a little taller somehow, his neck just a bit longer.

Grimm was talking some more about the Nazi past and the Nazi future. Once he got started, his few statements began to grow into an epistle. The first thing I wondered, listening to him, was if he was being so open about all of his Nazi bullshit because he had no intention of letting me leave the island alive. But then, the more I thought, I figured that he didn't care — that he was about to disappear with Brugmann and Tamm, and that he was so arrogant that it didn't matter what I knew.

He must have been talking for 30 seconds without a letup or even a pause to breathe. He was still going, and I figured, well, I don't know. But Grimm was preaching, and my eyes were locked on his, and my right hand began to creep toward my pocket, and...

"Don't even think about it." It was Hansi Brugmann. He was pointing a pistol at me. If I was stunned, Grimm was stunned, too.

"Right pocket," Brugmann said.

Grimm reached into my pocket and took my backup gun. It fit easily in his hand.

"Your mother's?" he said.

Grimm laughed. He shook his head.

"You really are a fucking amateur," he said.

The first shot, from somewhere behind me, exploded Brugmann's face like a dropped watermelon.

Grimm froze. Somehow, I managed to karate-chop his arm,

and the pistol — which he had been holding flat in his open hand as he mocked it — fell to the ground. We both dove for it, but I was able to get there first. I had it in my hand, but we were wrestling on the ground. Grimm held my arm, until he didn't. I managed to free it just enough to get a shot at a funny angle — funny but deadly. The bullet went through the bottom of Grimm's jaw and then up through his head. One shot from the lady gun had been enough.

Grimm fell on top of me, and it took some effort to extricate myself. When I did, I focused on Tamm. He was leaning over Hansi Brugmann's body, and then he stood up straight, and then he started running.

The second shot that Antti fired from his ancient revolver went through Karl Tamm's back, high up on his back. Whenever I told the story afterward, I said that Antti shot him in that freakish neck.

Tamm stopped after he had been hit and stood in place. He made a sound as if he had been choked — really loud, but only for a second. Then he fell where he was. He fell like a pole-axed giraffe.

50

I t took me nearly two weeks to get back to Vienna, by way of Stockholm, and I didn't tell anybody I was back. I didn't tell anybody until the coma, and then the week after the coma.

I was about to call Leon. Maybe one more day. He was my best friend and the closest thing I had to a therapist. I could tell him everything, every fucking thing, and he would have some advice. I had a big decision I needed to make, and, I don't know.

After a nap, I woke up to find an envelope shoved beneath my door. There was a card inside that said, "American Bar, 5 p.m." It was from Fritz Ritter, I knew.

There also was a newspaper clipping. The byline on the story was "From Our Scandinavia Correspondent."

Authorities in Helsinki said that the bodies of three men were found murdered yesterday on the island of Suomenlinna. The bodies were discovered by schoolchildren on a field trip to the island, which houses a derelict chain of fortresses that protected the city from attack in ancient times.

All three men were shot dead, and two of them were able to be identified. The first, Gerhard Grimm, lived in Helsinki and operated an import-export business in the city. The second, Hansi Brugmann, was a former captain in the German army who was convicted after the war of crimes related to his Nazi affiliations and jailed in Germany. Brugmann had reportedly died in prison in 1947. Inquiries made by a correspondent to German prison authorities about this discrepancy have not yet been answered.

The third victim has not yet been identified.

When I arrived at the American Bar, over near the cathedral, it was typically empty. Fritz was waiting for me, sipping at whatever. When I sat down, he shoved a Manhattan across the table.

He sipped, I sipped. And then Fritz said, "I didn't know. I promise you."

He sipped, I sipped. And if what he said made me feel better — I did believe him, at least partly because I had to believe him — I had already half made up my mind. I was willing to hear his side, but I didn't see how I was going to be able to keep working for the Gehlen Organization.

"First, tell me," he said, and I did. I went through the whole thing, filling in every detail I could remember from the time Fritz met me at the Kiek in de Kok until Antti dropped me off in Stockholm. I told him about Artur and I told him about Linna, even if I was telling on myself. He listened, and then he ordered two more drinks, and then he listened some more.

"I didn't know," he said, again.

"I believe you."

"We both got fucked. You worse than me, obviously, but we..."

"I know," I said. "I know."

I looked around the bar, stared down at the checkerboard floor, remembered happier times — before Gehlen and Fritz, before the war and middle age.

"I'm just back from Munich," Fritz said. "I saw the old man himself."

"The old man? Gehlen is older than you?"

"Well, maybe a year or two," he said, adding a shy smile. "I went to quit, to just fucking throw the whole thing in his face. He walked me through what happened — what he thinks happened. He swore he had no idea about Grimm's true loyalties, that he'd never done anything to give Gehlen any doubts. And the Brugmann thing, well, he promised he didn't know."

"Sounds like bullshit," I said.

"I don't think so."

"You hesitated. You're not sure."

"No, I'm not sure," he said.

We drank some more. Fritz had always told me that Gehlen was one of the good guys, and that he only hired the lowest-level former Nazis when he absolutely needed them as eyes and ears in the East. We had gone round and round over the years about this — and if I was more of a skeptic than Fritz, I still signed on. Eyes open and all that.

"So, you really resigned?"

"Kind of," Fritz said. "Gehlen told me to sleep on it, and that's where we left it. Part of me, well, you probably don't realize how guilty I feel. I trusted somebody, and he nearly got you killed. It's hard for me to live... I mean, I understand the dangers of the job. I've lived the dangers myself at times. I've sent people on assignments from which they didn't come back. That's bad enough. But to be duped, and to almost get you..."

He stopped and took a long drink.

"Part of me just wants to fucking run," Fritz said. "Just go plant petunias somewhere. Part of me, though, wants to stay. Staying might be the only good I can do in this world anymore, even if it's only to make sure that the Nazis aren't in control of what amounts to German national intelligence."

"What?"

"There's nobody else to do it," he said. "I mean, look around. It might not be official but, I mean, really. Look around. And if I can make sure that the Nazis don't..."

Another pause. Another long drink.

"And you?" he said.

Pause.

"I mean, if I stay?" Fritz said.

It was only after a long pause, and a long drink, that I finally admitted, "I just don't know."

ENJOY THIS BOOK? YOU CAN REALLY HELP ME OUT.

The truth is that, even as an author who has sold more than 200,000 books, it can be hard to get readers' attention. But if you have read this far, I have yours – and I could use a favor.

Reviews from people who liked this book go a long way toward convincing future readers of its worth. It won't take five minutes of your time, but it would mean a lot to me. Long or short, it doesn't matter.

Thanks!

I hope you enjoyed *Escape from Estonia,* the 11th installment in the Alex Kovacs thriller series. My other series, beginning with *A Death in East Berlin*, features a protagonist named Peter Ritter, a young murder detective in East Berlin at the time of the building of the Berlin Wall.

That book, as well as the rest of both series, is available for purchase now. You can find the links to all of my books at https://www.amazon.com/author/richardwake.

Thanks for your interest!